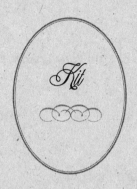

Also by Jane Peart

Orphan Train West for Young Adults
    Toddy
    Laurel
    Ivy and Allison
    April and May

Edgecliffe Manor Mysteries
    Web of Deception
    Shadow of Fear
    A Perilous Bargain
    Thread of Suspicion

Kit

Jane Peart

Fleming H. Revell
A Division of Baker Book House Co
Grand Rapids, Michigan 49516

Published by Fleming H. Revell
a division of Baker Book House Company
P.O. Box 6287, Grand Rapids, MI 49516-6287

Adapted from *Dreams of a Longing Heart,* published in 1990

Printed in the United States of America

Library of Congress Cataloging-in-Publication Data

Peart, Jane.
   Kit / Jane Peart.
       p. cm.
    "Adapted from Dreams of a longing heart, published in 1990"—
T.p. verso.
    Summary: Abandoned by her widowed father, Kit rides the Orphan Train west where a farm family takes her in to help with chores, never expecting that one day she would overcome all the obstacles before her and become a successful writer.
    ISBN 0-8007-5715-7 (pbk.)
    [1. Orphans—Fiction. 2. Christian life—Fiction.] I. Title.
PZ7.P32335 Ki 2000
[Fic]—dc21   99-042060

Scripture quotations are from the King James Version of the Bible.

For current information about all releases from Baker Book House, visit our web site:

http://www.bakerbooks.com

Boston, 1888

The early morning was dark and chilly, and the deserted street seemed to go on forever. Kit felt her toes push painfully against the end of her too-small leather boots. Several strides ahead of her she could see her father carrying her baby sister, her little round face bobbing over his broad shoulder.

"Get a move on, you two," Sean Ternan called to Kit and her little brother as he reached the top of the long hill. "Don't be laggin' behind. We're almost there."

Something cold and hard lodged in Kit's chest. She was the only one of the three children who knew where *there* was. Like Gwynny, Jamie didn't understand at all. But Kit did. She was seven years old, and her father had told her the night before. Kit brushed back a straggling strand of her brown hair. She remembered every word he had said.

"'Tis the only thing to do, Kit," he had explained as they sat at their tiny kitchen table. "There's no work for me here. I've got to go over to Brockton and see if I can get on at the shoe factory. They'll keep you until I find a place. Then I'll come back and get you."

"Why can't we come with you, Da?" Kit wanted to know. "It'll be Christmas soon. We can't be apart at Christmas."

Sean Ternan wiped his eyes and nose with a red handkerchief. "I don't have no choice. I don't even know if there'll be work there, Kit."

She knew what he meant. Sean Ternan, a bricklayer by trade, was from Ireland. In Boston, when the mills laid off workers, the Irish were the first to go. He had lost his job three months ago, not long after her mother's sickness and death. Times had been very hard since then.

"Kit, come along, girl!" Her father's voice echoed back along the empty street, jarring the youngster back into the frightening present. "We've not got all day."

"Come on, Jamie, it's not far now." She tugged at her brother's small hand.

"I'm hungry, Kit," the five-year-old whimpered, his breath visible like puffs of smoke.

Kit's own stomach felt hollow too. She hadn't been able to eat the watery oatmeal either.

"I'm cold too."

With that, Kit wanted to scold him and yell that she was hungry and cold too. But she couldn't. After all, he was only five, and he didn't understand.

The two of them trudged solemnly up the steep hill when suddenly she saw it. A black wrought iron arch loomed over a wide gate. At seven, Kit could read the sign: GREYSTONE COUNTY ORPHANAGE.

For the first time, something inside Kit rebelled. Almost frantically, she dashed forward, dragging Jamie with her. This couldn't be happening! *They* weren't orphans. They still had one parent, their Da! It wasn't right. It wasn't fair.

Kit slipped her chilly fingers into her father's big workman's hand for comfort. He held on to it, but he didn't look at her. Instead, he looked straight ahead to the huge paneled door in front of them. Slowly he pulled the long bell cord, and Kit could hear the distant sound of ringing from deep inside.

A thin, gray-haired woman opened the door and peered at them over her small half glasses.

"Yes?"

"I'm Sean Ternan," he replied, taking off his cap. "These are my children."

Kit heard her father's words as if from far away. Before she knew it, she was standing beside him in a room with a high ceiling.

"'Tis only temporary, Miss Clinock." Mr. Ternan twisted his woolen cap nervously while Gwynny perched on his lap sucking her thumb. "As soon as I've found work, I intend to come back for my family."

The severe-looking woman with the high-necked blouse was now seated behind a desk. "Of course you understand we can only give temporary shelter for six months, Mr. Ternan. If they're not reunited with you by then, we'll be forced to seek a suitable adoptive home for them. Our institution is almost full now."

Kit felt scared. Jamie fidgeted at her side. Then she heard the creak of the door opening behind them.

"These are the Ternan children," Miss Clinock announced.

In walked a heavyset woman in a black dress and gray apron. The woman filled the doorway.

"The little girl goes to nursery, the boy to primary and—" Miss Clinock paused, her eyes staring over her half glasses at Kit. "How old are you, child?"

"Seven," Kit murmured shyly.

"Speak up, now. Don't mumble."

"She's near eight," her father chimed in quickly. "Smart as a whip too."

"All right, then, take her to third," Miss Clinock directed.

Kit felt strong fingers clamp on her thin shoulders, spinning her around like a top toward the door. With Jamie's hand in hers, Kit started forward. Her father lifted Gwynny out of his lap and gently shoved her toward the stranger.

"Take her hand, Kit. She'll go with you."

Everything inside her screamed no! This was a mistake. A very BIG mistake! Surely Da would scoop the three of them up and go. Surely he wouldn't leave them in this scary place.

Instead, Sean Ternan sat there as rigid as a rock. He didn't move, nor did he offer his oldest daughter even one word of hope. Instead, his eyes were locked on the woolen cap he kept twisting between his fingers.

"Good-bye, Da!" Kit called over her shoulder. "Good-bye!"

Shy, Kit had a hard time making friends at first. However, one little girl with red-gold curly hair and round blue eyes sat on the other side of the double desk during school time. Her real name was Victorine Zephronia

Todd, but everyone called her Toddy. The fun-loving Toddy instantly took the newcomer under her wing, explaining how things worked and making jokes about everything she explained. The two became fast friends. Before long, a third little girl named Laurel Vestal arrived. Within a few days they had welcomed her, and she made the group a threesome. Like the Three Musketeers, Kit, Laurel, and Toddy became inseparable.

The days ticked into weeks at the orphanage. Each girl wore the same uniform, a blue muslin pinafore buttoned over a coarse cotton dress. Kit had finally gotten used to the itchy black woolen stockings and sturdy black shoes laced to the ankles. The drab routine was the same for everyone too. The children stood in line for their meals, attended school classes, had recess on the stark playground, and slept on narrow hard cots in a dormitory room. On Sundays after chapel service, they were allowed to play with one another and visit any brothers or sisters on the playground. Kit looked forward to Sundays because she could see Jamie and their two-year-old sister, Gwynny.

One Sunday during recess, Kit, Toddy, and Laurel were playing jump rope in the fenced-in playground. A single towering oak tree full of red-tipped leaves basked in the afternoon sun that peeked through the cottony clouds. A pair of gray squirrels played tag around its thick trunk.

"Come look!" someone yelled.

The group rushed over to the wire fence in time to see an elegant horse-drawn carriage pull up in front of the main entrance. A well-dressed couple got out and went inside.

"Who do you think they are?" Toddy's turned-up nose pressed against the wire mesh.

"Somebody's parents coming to get them," Laurel replied, rubbing a dirty smudge off her rosy cheek.

"No, stupid!" It was Molly B., the class bully. "They're folks come to visit the nursery and pick out a baby."

"What do you mean?" Kit asked, turning toward her.

The chunky red-haired girl snickered. "Just what I said, ninny. They're gonna take a baby home with them. They always pick the little ones."

Kit felt her stomach lurch. Surely they wouldn't let Gwynny be adopted! Not when their Da was coming back to get them soon. She scrunched her eyes shut and pursed her lips in obvious pain.

"Bet your little sister'll be adopted," Molly smirked.

"What do you know?" Toddy had already grabbed Kit's arm and was leading her away from the fence.

"I been here longer than you! I know." Molly's taunting voice trailed behind them.

Later that afternoon, Kit sat down on one of the stone benches to wait for her weekly visit with her brother and sister.

When her brother arrived, she asked, "Jamie, where's Gwynny?"

"Dunno," the boy replied, drawing a figure in the sand with a stick. "I heard the nursery lady say she was on a probation visit."

Kit's heart jolted. "What's that?" she gasped.

Jamie shook his head. "That's all she said."

Kit grabbed her little brother by the shoulders. "What's the matter with you, Jamie?" She shook him. "Why didn't you ask? That's our Gwynny she was talking about. Now we don't know where she is!"

"Leggo of me, Kit! You're hurting me!" The five-year-old wriggled out of her grip.

His sister let her arms drop. "I'm sorry, Jamie. I didn't mean to hurt you," she said, blinking back tears. "But we've got to find out. What if Da comes to get us?"

"Da's not coming back," Jamie mumbled.

"That's a wicked thing to say," Kit scolded. "Da *is* coming back."

"No, he's not, Kit. My friend Tommy says so. He says we aren't temporary anymore because we've been here too long. He says those people that came by today probably got Gwynny."

A scratchy lump now stuck in her throat like dry crusty bread. It had been months since their father had brought them here. She had tried to keep track of the time, but she had somehow gotten mixed up. Da had left them last Christmas. It had been December 1888. But what month was it now? The leaves on the old oak were turning, so it had to be fall. Kit counted on her fingers. One . . . two . . . three . . . She grimaced. They *had* been at Greystone longer than six months.

"Can I go play now?"

Kit watched her brother disappear through the primary gate. Suddenly an awful fear clutched her young heart. Would she ever see him again?

Two weeks later, Kit found out that Jamie had been adopted too.

"What will my Da say when he comes and they're not here?" Kit demanded tearfully as she stood in front of Miss Clinock's desk.

"Your father signed the papers, Kit," the head matron replied. "He agreed to their adoptions."

Kit gulped. "Then is he comin' for *me?*" she finally managed to ask.

"I'm sorry, Kit, but I'm afraid not."

Kit's heart shattered into a thousand pieces that day. She had lost her mother and her sister and brother. Now her Da too. And if he didn't want her, who would?

Meadowridge

Cora Hansen lifted the heavy blue enamel coffeepot from the potbellied stove to refill her husband's cup. Jess was scraping the last of the pork sausage and fried eggs onto his fork with a jellied biscuit.

"You'll be sure to quit afore noon so's we can eat and get into town in time, won't ya?" the woman asked anxiously. She was still worried that he would change his mind.

Not one to talk much, the sour-faced farmer continued to chew.

"Jess? You didn't forget, did you? Today's the day the Orphan Train gets here. We need to get into town early so's we can look 'em over good."

Married for fifteen years, Mrs. Hansen looked a good deal older than her thirty-five years. Her straight mousy hair was pulled back into a tight knot, and her skin looked like wrinkled paper from years of working in the sun. A flowered housedress drooped over thin bony shoulders, and her spindly hands were busy as bees every minute of the day.

The life of a farmer's wife was taking a toll on Cora, and she knew it. Bringing up five strapping, active boys didn't help matters either. Her two older sons, Lonny and Casper, were nine and ten, but they worked with their father out in the fields each day. The three younger boys couldn't do much for her except gather eggs and feed the chickens. Cora had to do the rest by herself.

That was why the idea of adopting an orphan girl had appealed to her so much. A girl could help. She could churn the butter, mix the bread dough, hang laundry on wash day. She could pluck chickens and pick squash or corn for dinner. Cora would even teach her to can and sew. Yep, it would be like unloading a wagon full of bricks. A good strong girl would lighten Cora's load considerably.

Jess wiped his greasy mouth with the back of a veined hand, then pushed the caned chair back from the table. He glared at his wife.

"Don't seems to me we need no other child 'round here, Cora," he grunted. "And besides, I'll lose pretty near a day's work goin' to town to fetch her."

Cora wiped her sun-spotted hands on her blue-checkered apron. She had worked all her life, from the time she had helped her brothers while her pa unsuccessfully prospected the hills around Meadowridge until she had married Jess, a widower. She squared her hunched shoulders. Cora wasn't about to give up. She needed the help and that was all there was to it.

"I told ya, Jess. It'll be another pair of hands. There's enough work 'round here for two women. I mean to pick out a half-growed girl, strong, sturdy. She'll be a big help. You'll see." Cora tried to keep her voice from trembling.

She knew that if Jess got his mind set the other way, she'd never be able to change it back.

Her husband's sun-weathered face wore a permanent scowl, his narrow eyes and down-turned mouth gave evidence of a stubborn man made bitter by the hardships of a farmer's life.

Jess stood up. "We gots to sign some papers, don't we? Put money out?"

"No, Jess," his wife quickly replied. "The man from the Boston Rescuers and Providers' Society said we jest gots to feed and dress her and see she gits her schoolin' 'til she's eighteen. So, we don't have to do nothin' else. That's all there is to it."

Jess took his straw hat from the hook beside the kitchen door and placed it on his head. The hinges squeaked on the back screen door as he pushed it open. "Got to oil this afore too long," he grumbled. "I got my hands full with the farm and livestock, Cora. Cain't take on nothin' more."

"She'll pull her weight, Jess," Cora replied loud enough so her voice would follow him onto the back porch. "I'll see to that."

It was getting light now. Soon the boys would be scrambling down the stairs for breakfast. Cora's wooden spoon stirred the simmering oatmeal in a deep iron pot. She wondered what it would be like to have another female around the house. Cora had always felt like an outsider, as if she weren't good enough for the likes of some of those uppity Meadowridge folks. It gave her a smug feeling to know she would be one of the families willing to offer shelter to one of the poor abandoned orphans from the East.

Not that she had gone to a lot of trouble getting ready for her. She had cleared out the clutter from a corner of the tiny attic to make a sleeping room. After cleaning an old iron bedstead, she had covered it with limp muslin sheets and a white coverlet. It wasn't much, but it was probably better than this girl was used to. Besides, the child would learn soon enough that the Hansens were simple farmers living in a simple frame house on a simple farm in Meadowridge, Arkansas.

The trip across the country from Boston had been long and tiring. Meadowridge was the last of the four stops for the Orphan Train. Kit stared out the grimy window as the train slowed down just outside their final destination. Horses and cattle dotted the rolling green hills and meadows. Lush farmland with the tilled black soil of spring formed a patchwork quilt in front of her eyes. How very different this looked from the dreary streets and cold stone buildings in Boston.

At first, Kit was glad she had listened to Toddy and pretended to be crippled during the stops along the way. The three friends had been willing to do anything to stay close together, so they had formed a plan. Kit would turn her foot sideways and limp. Laurel would hunch her shoulders up into a monstrous position and twist her mouth. Toddy would try to keep her big blue eyes crossed. It had worked too. No one had selected them.

But now, doubts crowded the youngster's mind. It was 1890, and she was nine years old now. Would anyone want her? She was plain and tall and skinny. Even her own Da hadn't wanted her; he had abandoned her. Had God forgotten her too? As the locomotive pulled to a stop in front of the yellow frame Meadowridge depot, Kit prayed, *Please, Lord, I don't want to be left behind again.*

A short while later, she sat on a straight-backed chair placed along a wall in the Meadowridge Community Church social hall. The ladies of the church had laid out a banquet of food for the occasion. Platters of fried chicken and sliced ham and bowls of coleslaw and potato salad beckoned for people to help themselves. Homemade bread still warm from the oven and all sorts of berry pies and cakes covered the blue-checkered tablecloths. This was a far cry from the diet of crackers and dried apples she had received on the train.

With her empty plate still on her lap, Kit watched Toddy leave in the company of an elegantly dressed elderly woman and a girl about twelve years old. Then she saw Laurel go out hand-in-hand with the nice doctor who had given each of them a quick physical examination. Her two friends must have already found homes. *What about me?* Kit wondered.

With her cardboard suitcase at her feet, she was feeling very lonely.

All at once, Anna Scott said, "Come along, Kit. You've been adopted." She held out her hand.

Anna Scott was married to the man who had organized the Orphan Train. She had taken care of the girls during the trip.

Kit jumped up from her chair. "I have?" She could hardly believe her ears. Maybe her prayer was being answered after all!

"Yes. You're going with the Hansen family. They live on a farm just outside Meadowridge. Isn't that nice?"

Back in Boston, Kit had read stories about farms. They had always sounded so nice, and the farmers had been so kind. Now she was going to live on one. This was exciting!

Mrs. Scott led her over to a tall man standing with Pastor Scott on the other side of the room. The man wore blue denim overalls with patched knees. His stubby chin needed a shave, and his thinning gray hair looked greasy and matted. As they approached, Kit clutched onto Mrs. Scott's hand.

"This is Kathleen Ternan, Mr. Hansen," Mrs. Scott introduced her. "She's called Kit."

Without a word, the gruff farmer nodded then stuffed some papers into his overall pocket. "Well, then, let's git goin'."

Mrs. Scott bent down to cup Kit's worried face in her hands. "You'll be fine, sweetheart," she said. "Don't worry. Mrs. Hansen has five boys. I'm sure she's looking forward to having a sweet child like you."

Kit wasn't sure she wanted to go with this grim-looking man at all, even if he was a farmer and did live on a farm. With her suitcase in her hands, she hesitated.

"Come on!" The farmer stood frowning in the open doorway.

Mrs. Scott gave her a final hug. "Go ahead, Kit, and God bless you."

Once outside, Mr. Hansen untied the mare from the hitching post and climbed up into the buckboard seat. "Well, come on, girl, git in!"

Things hadn't gone right for Jess all day. This morning, he had discovered that one of the boys had left the pasture gate open. It took him the good part of an hour to round up the three cows that had gotten out. Upset with the delay, Cora had banged the pots and pans so much during the noon meal that he'd gotten a headache. Then, when Seth had dumped a bowl of soaking lima beans all over himself, Cora had been forced to stay home to clean up the mess. "Now you see why I needs the help!" were his wife's last harsh words before he left.

Now, to make matters worse, he knew Cora was going to be mad as a wet hen when she saw the size of the girl. A string bean of a girl who could be blown away by one strong wind. A lot of help this one would be! And to think, he'd given up a whole morning of plowing. The man sighed. Well, Cora would just have to take what she got.

"You deaf, girl? I said, git in."

Struggling with her heavy suitcase, the little girl grabbed the handle on the side of the wagon and hoisted herself up. Her straw bonnet slid off and was dangling by its ribbons around her neck. But before she could tie it, Mr. Hansen flicked the reins and the open wagon jerked forward. Kit gripped the side of the seat to keep her balance.

The wagon rumbled along, stirring up a cloud of dust from the packed dirt street leading away from the depot. It passed an arched stone bridge over a long winding river with willow trees gracing the banks. On the other side, Kit could see neat clapboard houses with pretty gardens and picket fences. On top of the high hill overlooking the town sat a beautiful Victorian house with a peaked roof and balconies.

Growing up in the grimy, industrial New England city of Boston, Kit was used to air that smelled like a factory. But here in Meadowridge, blossoming apple trees beside the road delicately scented the country air, leaving a pure clean feeling. Kit took in a long deep breath.

The mare's harness jangled as they headed out of town. Following the river, the road narrowed, and Kit observed the surrounding countryside. To her right, a herd of cattle grazed on the bladed grass of a meadow. A few cows glanced up as the wagon passed by. On the sloping hillside to her left, three white lambs frolicked.

Kit started to point at the scenery but then caught herself. The man next to her had not said a word. His rough hands snapped the reins every now and then, but he sat there glumly. So Kit kept her excitement to herself, and the two of them rode on in silence.

In the meantime, Cora had been to the kitchen window at least a dozen times, searching for some sign of her husband's return. As if it wasn't bad enough being stuck at home, she had bitten her fingernails to the quick while waiting. This was too important to mess up. Finally, she spotted the wagon in the distance and rushed out on the front porch stoop.

Without looking toward the house, Jess reined his mare to a stop. He jumped down and waited while a thin, pale child clambered down from the other side of the high front seat.

"Is *that* her?" Casper's high-pitched voice spoke Cora's unspoken thoughts. He and his four curious brothers hid behind her, tugging at her checkered apron.

What in the world was this? Cora couldn't believe what she was seeing. Why, this young'un didn't look any bigger than a minute. She wouldn't be fit to hang the laundry much less haul in buckets of water from the well. What could Jess have been thinking? He must have been plumb out of his mind to take this one.

Cora watched as the orphan awkwardly toted her cumbersome suitcase around the front of the buggy and across the gravel drive. Then, from the bottom step, a pair of wide gray eyes looked up at her. The sweetness of a smile, revealing a narrow space between two front teeth, momentarily unsettled Cora and tugged at her heart. Just as quickly, she spoke gruffly. "Well, you might as well come in. Supper's near ready." She turned abruptly and shoved her gawking boys back through the front screen door.

Kit followed Mrs. Hansen through the front hall and up some narrow steps to the unfinished third floor.

"Up here's your place." The woman was already headed back down the stairs. "When you've washed up, you can come down and eat."

Breathless from the climb, Kit dropped her suitcase onto the bare floor and looked around. Under the low slanted ceiling was a single, black iron bed with a thin white coverlet and a neatly folded striped blanket. On top of a four-drawer knotty pine chest was a white pottery washbowl and pitcher. Over it hung a tiny unframed oval mirror. A wooden rack held a yellow washcloth and two clean but worn green towels. Kit could scarcely believe it. She had never before had a room to herself.

She crept over to the small bench under the eave and unlatched the window and gently pushed it open. The sweet fresh air smelled like a precious perfume. The sun's afternoon rays just touched the treetops, bathing them in a golden haze. She could see the pasture and fields and, way in the distance, that same long river winding its way from Meadowridge. It was more beautiful than she could ever have imagined. Oh, how blessed she was to be here!

From the start, Kit felt very lonely at times. She missed Laurel and Toddy dreadfully. But the threesome did get to see one another once a week during Sunday school at the Meadowridge Community Church.

It was there that Kit learned about Toddy and Laurel. Toddy had been adopted by the woman in black who owned the big Victorian house on the top of the hill. Mrs. Olivia Hale had an invalid granddaughter named Helene, who was very kind to Toddy. Toddy was growing to love Helene and seemed very happy. Laurel now lived with Dr. Woodward and his wife in town. She had told Kit that Mrs. Woodward was sad because she had lost her own little girl some time ago. But all in all, Laurel was happy too.

In spite of Mr. Hansen's dislike of social events, he told his family they could attend the town's annual Fourth of July picnic this year. His wife jumped at the chance and got ready. She eagerly rolled the thin pie crust for two of her delicious cherry pies and baked a carrot cake with lots of raisins. One of the hams came up from the cellar, and on the morning of the picnic, Cora and Kit were up at dawn, packing the family's wicker hamper.

"When are we goin'?" Casper whined as he and Lonny sparred with one another in the kitchen.

"When I'm good and ready!" Cora snapped as she finished wrapping a cloth towel around a warm loaf of freshly baked cinnamon bread. "Quit that jostlin' and go git in the wagon, or ya won't go at all."

The screen door crashed open as the two boys thundered outside. Kit stood quietly near the pantry, awaiting directions. She had learned not to ask too much. Her new mother did not like many questions.

"Well, I 'spose that's it. Iffen we forgot sumthin', it'll have to be forgot."

Cora pulled her green knit shawl from its peg on the door, tied on her bonnet, and motioned to Kit. Together, they carried the hamper out to the wagon.

All the way into town, Kit excitedly looked forward to seeing her two friends, who would be there too. By the time the Hansens arrived, tethered horses and open buggies jammed the large meadow near the church. Blankets of all sizes peppered the landscape as people everywhere settled with their picnic lunches. Jess found them a place near a tall red maple.

Kit loved the day, especially when Laurel invited her to have dessert with her and the Woodwards. Amazingly, Cora agreed. The two delighted girls scampered off together.

A short while later, Cora was packing some leftovers in the picnic basket as Jess chomped on his last fried chicken leg. The boys were playing a game of tag nearby. When a shadow fell across the blanket, Cora looked up to see Ava Woodward.

"It's nice to see you, Mrs. Hansen." Her voice was soft.

Squinting her eyes against the glare of the sun, Cora wondered what the highfalutin doctor's wife could possibly want.

Ava went on. "The girls are having such a good time that I thought we might let them spend the rest of the day together, if it's all right with you. This evening Leland and I are taking Laurel up to Olivia's house to watch the fireworks. We'd love to have Kit join us."

"Well, ma'am, that's mighty nice of ya," Cora said stiffly. "But jest 'cause today's a holiday don't mean there ain't no chores. Kit needs to come back and do her work."

Cora's boys would have thrown fits if the same thing had happened to them. All the way back to the farm, Cora watched for some sign that the little girl might be disappointed or upset, but she never saw one. When they returned home, the child did exactly as she was told without a word.

A few weeks later, Kit was hanging out laundry. She shook out a damp sheet from the heaping pile in the huge oak-chip basket. Stretching up her arms, she pinned it to the hemp rope clothesline stretched between the house and a wooden post near the fence. With the back of one hand, she wiped some beads of perspiration from her brow.

All morning she had been helping Cora with the washing, starting right after breakfast. First, she lugged buckets of water from the outside well into the house, pouring each one into a big cast-iron pot on the stove. Then Cora posted her at the stove to watch until the water began to boil. When that happened, she lifted the heavy pot off the stove and took it outside, where Cora was bent over a wide copper tub set on a wooden sawhorse. There, Cora scrubbed the soiled overalls and shirts, undergarments and linen on a long metal washboard.

When each load was done, Cora piled it into the oversized basket so Kit could hang the clothes on the clothesline. It was hot heavy work on this warm summer day.

As Kit pinned another wet sheet on the line, she thought about her life with the Hansens.

Mealtimes were silent in this household. This seemed very strange to a child who had spent her early life in an Irish family where mealtime was talk time. There never seemed to be any laughter here either. Kit missed her friend Toddy, who always made her laugh. On the other hand, tricks and teasing were a way of life at the Hansen farm. Casper and Lonny were the main culprits, Kit their target.

One night not long after she arrived, the two pranksters snuck up to her attic room and packed a tiny live frog in the toe of one of her high-top shoes. The next morning she could hear laughter through the cracks in the floorboard when she shrieked as the slimy thing wiggled at the end of her toes. Another time, the two stashed a dead mouse in her pitcher. When she went to pour out some water, its stiff, smelly carcass plunked into the unsuspecting washbowl. Kit couldn't even pick vegetables in the garden without having to watch over her shoulder to make sure the mischievous boys weren't getting ready to kick over her full basket or set the cross old rooster out to chase her. She never knew when or how the next attack was coming.

However, the younger Hansens, Chet, Tom, and Seth, seemed to be warming to her. Not long after the Fourth of July, the three had come down with the measles. To help them pass the time, Kit had read to them from a book she had found in the attic. Now, the young'uns tugged and begged until she read to them each day. They would scramble onto her lap or plop down on the floor and listen quietly to Kit's wonderful stories. Kit quickly discovered she was enjoying the time as much as they were.

The clean sheets were finally hanging on the line. As Kit snatched up the empty basket, she looked back. The linen swayed gently back and forth as if an invisible hand were swinging it. As she reached the back steps, however, Kit heard a wild peal of laughter. She whirled around to see what was so funny.

There lay all the beautiful clean sheets, crumpled in the dry clay on top of a fallen clothesline. Two overalled figures were running fast toward the barn.

Kit instantly dropped the basket and took off, her pigtails flying behind her head in the breeze. "Just you wait!" she screamed. "I'll get you both!"

Within seconds, she had flown across the yard and rounded the barn. A few chickens scratched at the dirt and pecked at the bugs. The boys were nowhere in sight. Kit blinked back angry tears. What could she do? With sagging shoulders, she headed back toward the house.

Just then, the back screen door banged against the house as Cora flung it open.

"Land sakes, girl!" she exclaimed. "Cain't you even hang up clothes proper?" The woman pursed her thin lips. "Didn't they teach you nuthin' in that orphanage?"

The days grew a bit cooler as August flowed into September. Late one afternoon, her arms piled high with outgrown clothes, Cora climbed up the narrow steps to the attic. At the top, sunlight filtered through the tiny window to show dust particles on the rough plank floor. Cora discovered Kit writing something.

"Didn't know you was up here, Kit." Cora breathed heavily. The climb had winded her.

"Can I help?" the child offered, setting aside her pencil.

Cora nodded. Her back was hurting again. It seemed to hurt a lot these days, so she always welcomed the help. The two of them placed the pants and shirts into the large musty trunk at the far end.

As she closed the heavy lid, Cora's eyes swept the room. Kit certainly kept the place neat, even made her bed every morning. Everything looked nice and tidy.

But something was different. What was it? Cora scanned the room again.

Then she spotted it. A small framed picture of an angel hovering over a little boy and girl who were crossing a rickety bridge had been tacked to the bare wall beside Kit's bed.

"Where'd you get that?" she asked, pointing to the picture.

"It was a prize at Sunday school," Kit answered.

Cora was amazed. The little girl had won a prize and never told a soul! Her young'uns would have whooped and hollered until the man in the moon had patted them on their heads. What kind of child was this anyway?

"Teacher give it to ya?"

"No, ma'am, I picked it out." Kit hesitated a moment. "It reminded me of my little brother and sister."

Cora could feel her chest tighten. Without a word, she turned away and scurried back down the stairs. What was the matter with her? The attic wasn't that hot today, at least not enough to make her feel faint. She walked onto the back porch for some air.

Cora stood there for a moment thinking about Kit and her own childhood. Then she walked back inside to her bedroom on the first floor. There at the foot of the four-poster bed was an old trunk. Cora knelt down and carefully undid the rusty latches to open the lid.

She dug through the trunk until she found what she wanted and gently brought out a crocheted afghan with zigzag stripes. She held the soft colorful blanket in her lap, running her gnarled hands across its softness. It had taken her an entire winter to finish this piece, and then she had never used it. Cora was never quite sure why. Jess preferred quilts at night, and she didn't have any women friends who might admire it. Maybe that was it, she thought. Before her mind persuaded her otherwise, Cora raised herself up and marched back to the attic.

"Here, you might like this to put over your bed," she said as she handed the afghan to Kit.

"Oh, thank you!" the little girl exclaimed.

For the first time, the woman smiled at the child. Something inside Cora had been frozen for many years. Somehow, this little orphan was bringing it back to life. Like the hard earth in spring after a cold harsh winter, Cora's heart was beginning to thaw.

A few days later, she was stirring the bubbling contents of a hot kettle on the stove. Blackberry jam would come in handy this winter on buckwheat cakes and biscuits, she thought. Can't let anything go to waste on a farm. She lifted a spoonful of the dark purple liquid and examined it, then let it drip back into the pot. No, still not thick enough. Maybe she should let Kit do the stirring for a while instead of having her outside picking the last of the summer squash.

She glanced out the window over the kitchen sink. She could see the little girl bent over working in the garden. As her wooden spoon went round and round, Cora thought about the past few months.

It was sure different having a girl around. Restful like. Her boys were always making a racket, pushing, shoving, wrestling each other. But this little girl was as quiet as a kitten napping in the summer sun, yet always right there when Cora needed her. Caught on real quick too, and Cora liked that.

Kit was a good girl. Minded. Didn't sass. Did her chores and whatever else Cora told her without a fuss. She hadn't even gotten upset over missing that Fourth of

July thing. Somehow, Cora felt bad about that now. She should have let Kit go that day.

Early that evening, Cora found an assortment of colorful wildflowers in a vase on the kitchen table. Kit must have picked them earlier in the day. The child had placed daisies, purple wild asters, and Queen Anne's lace in a wide-necked green bottle full of water. Cora decided right off that she liked the looks of it.

At dinner, however, not everyone agreed.

"Who put them weeds in here?" Jess growled. "Makes my nose itch."

Casper clapped his hand over his mouth.

"Weeds!" Lonny hollered, jabbing his finger in the air. "Lookit them weeds!"

Sitting to Cora's left, Kit's face turned scarlet, like a ripe strawberry.

"Betcha she thinks they're beautiful, jest like them cows!" hooted Casper.

Jess could be rude and downright mean at times, but enough was enough. Cora jumped to Kit's defense. "I think they look right pretty, Jess." Then, turning to the boys, she snapped, "And I suggest you boys jest keep yer opinion to yerself."

A short while later, she and Kit were clearing away the dinner plates.

"School'll be startin' soon," Cora said matter-of-factly as she stacked the dirty plates. "I got a piece of flowered calico put back that'd make a dress."

"Thank you," Kit replied, picking up a platter of cornbread crumbs. "I'd like that very much."

Nothing else was said. Nothing else needed to be said.

Over time, Kit grew accustomed to the hard life at the Hansen farm. But she never quite got used to Jess. He had hardly said a word to her since she arrived. His manner remained gruff and his attitude was always grouchy. Sensitive Kit shied away from Jess Hansen. She was afraid of him.

One day the back door slammed open as Cora was shelling peas for supper and Kit was filling the kettle at the kitchen pump.

"Well, that cat's gettin' pretty old." Jess tossed his battered straw hat on the peg near the door. "Reckon this'll be her last litter. Guess I'll keep one and drown the rest."

Kit nearly dropped the kettle.

The man's words chilled Kit's heart. "Got that burlap bag out back. I'll jest weight it down and throw them in the river."

How could he do such a thing? Kit knew the surly farmer's cruel streak. She had seen Casper and Lonny duck from the back side of his swift strong hand. She had noticed their red eyes and blue welts after going with their father into the woodshed. She herself had been the object of his tirades. But they were all people and they could withstand it. The kittens were poor defenseless creatures who only wanted to love and be loved!

Before Kit could stop herself, she cried out, "No, you can't!"

Jess glowered at her. "We don't need more'n one cat."

But Kit couldn't help herself. She had watched the kittens being born. She had sat on a bale of hay while the mother licked and cleaned her babies. She had stroked their tiny bodies and had fallen in love with them. The thought that anyone would drown those adorable creatures was horrifying.

She gave Cora a pleading glance, but Cora was busy.

"Oh, please! Let me see if I can find homes for them before you do anything!" Kit begged.

To Kit's surprise, Cora spoke up. "There ain't no real hurry, is there, Jess?" She wiped her hands on a towel. "Why not let her try?"

Jess scowled. "We'll have to wait 'til they're weaned. Don't know as I wants to do that."

"A week or ten days ain't goin' to matter that much." Jess jammed his hands in his overall pockets and stomped back outside. The screen door banged behind him.

"Oh, thank you, Mrs. Hansen!" Kit wanted to hug Cora, but she didn't.

"You better do like you said, girl," Cora advised. "I don't fancy buckin' Jess when he's set his mind on somethin'."

As it turned out, the smallest of the litter died. But Kit found homes for the three others. Toddy and her new sister, Helene, each took a kitten, and the Woodwards gave Laurel permission to bring one home as well. That left one for Kit, a tawny male she named Ginger. Each night without Jess's knowledge, Ginger slept curled up at the foot of Kit's bed. He had become Kit's very own pet.

Standing up to Jess had helped Kit face some of her fears about him. He might be as gruff as an old mule, but he could be persuaded. This incident also made Kit aware that Cora was really on her side. An unspoken bond was being forged like a chain linking the two of them. And while Kit didn't understand it all, she knew it was special.

5

From her desk, Miss Millicent Cady looked over her third-grade classroom. The windows were open to a gentle May breeze. Outside, bees buzzed around the pink buds of the nearby apple trees while robins and blue jays flew among the branches. She was finding it hard to concentrate today. Spring fever!

The children had it too. Every few minutes one student or another would glance up from his or her workbook and gaze longingly outside. Milly smiled. Maybe she should ring the bell early today and dismiss them. After all, what harm would it do for one day?

This year at Meadowridge Grammar School had been a good one. As Milly tapped her pencil on the paper she was grading, she thought about her reservations last fall. Like many others, she had not known how the Orphan Train children were going to fit in. In fact, she had been rather worried about it. How foolish she had been! Kit, Laurel, and Toddy had proven valuable additions to the class.

Especially Kit. Miss Cady had discovered that Kit Ternan was an exceptional student with a flair for writing. The teacher had concerns about the Hansen family however. They had never shown any interest in their boys' education, and she was certain they didn't care about Kit's either. Jess Hansen had been to the school only once and that was to tell her he would whip his boys good if they didn't learn their "'rithmetic."

Milly had determined early on that she was going to nourish Kit's thirst for knowledge. She introduced Kit to the town library and even invited her to borrow books from her own bookcase at home.

Just then, the third grader looked up from her work and smiled, her clear eyes sparkling. Miss Cady smiled back.

Kit's fingers tightened around her pencil as she looked back down at her paper. Her mind had wandered away from the multiplication problem as if it were a wayward horse. She was thinking about Miss Cady.

The youngster liked Miss Cady so much and wanted to be just like her when she grew up. After all, teachers could read as many books as they wanted and live in cute little cottages with flowers in their gardens.

Kit had been in Miss Cady's house twice, and she had loved it. It was so different from the Hansens' plain farmhouse. The teacher had a small polished woodstove in her spotless kitchen and a little round table covered with a crisp linen cloth embroidered with red roses. During Kit's visits, Miss Cady had served her real tea in pink china cups and delicious wedges of thin cinnamon toast. Kit had knelt for a long time in front of the parlor bookcase trying to make up her mind about which books she was going to borrow.

Maybe it wasn't right to dream about such things, but Kit secretly wished she had been adopted by Miss Cady.

School was a welcome relief from the joyless routine on the farm. Kit had to get up before dawn to do her chores and then trudge to the gate where a group of children waited to ride into town on the milk wagon. When she got home in the afternoon, there were always more chores, more meals to prepare, more ironing and sewing and canning. The jobs never seemed to end.

Suddenly, the school bell clanged and everyone jumped.

"Early dismissal today, boys and girls," Miss Cady announced smiling.

Pencils dropped and workbooks slammed shut. The room emptied as if by magic as everyone quickly scampered out. Only Kit remained. She walked up to Miss Cady, who was erasing their homework assignment from the chalkboard.

"Miss Cady," she spoke quietly, "I'd like to ask you about the composition tablets."

"Yes, Kit, what is it?"

The child's dark lashes set off her wide gray eyes. Her brown hair framed her delicate ivory skin. "I noticed that most of them still have a few pages left even though we finished our last essay for the year."

Milly stopped erasing.

"I wondered if I could have the leftover blank pages."

The teacher placed the eraser on the chalky tray. "I don't see why not," she replied. "I was going to throw them away anyway. But I'm curious, Kit. Why do you want them?"

The little girl's eyes lowered and her cheeks turned the color of a pink rose. "I want to use them to write to my little brother and sister," she answered quietly.

"I didn't realize you had a brother and sister, Kit." Milly was amazed. "Where do they live?"

The youngster shook her braided head. "I don't know, Miss Cady. You see, they were adopted, and I don't know where they're placed. But someday, when I'm grown up, I'm going to try to find them." Kit shuffled from one foot to the other. "For now, I write them letters telling them about what I'm doing."

"If you'll wait a minute, Kit, I'll help you tear out the pages."

Later that afternoon after she had finished her chores, Kit settled herself comfortably by the window. Ginger had wrapped himself into a ball on her pillow, and she could hear his contented purr. Kit smoothed out a sheet of new paper and began to write:

Dear Jamie and Gwynny,

School is nearly out for the year. I got promoted to the fourth grade, and Miss Cady is going to be my teacher again. I am so glad! I think I will be a teacher like her when I grow up. Or maybe a writer. I hope I can live in a pretty little cottage too. I wish you could see my little cat Ginger. He's really growing. I get to play with him each night before I go to bed. I miss you both and wish we were together. I hope you don't forget me.

Your loving sister,
Kit

The Class of 1900

With her arms full of books, Kit threaded her way through the group of students sitting on the front steps of Meadowridge High School. She was already late for her job at the library, so she was in a hurry, but as she passed the tennis courts, she heard her name.

"Kit! Wait!"

Dressed in a white tennis blouse and matching skirt, Toddy dashed out through the wire-mesh door of the court. Her fiery red-gold hair was damp with perspiration. She had been playing doubles with Laurel and their friends, Chris Blanchard and Dan Brooks. Kit could see the other three volleying the ball back and forth.

"Can you stay overnight after the awards banquet?" Toddy panted, trying to catch her breath.

"I haven't asked Cora yet, Toddy," Kit replied, switching her books to the other arm. "But I will when I go out to the farm this weekend."

"She'll have to say yes, Kit. After all, it's part of graduation week." Her friend whirled her tennis racket between her two hands as they talked.

"I know, but we bake on Saturdays and she—"

"You can't miss it, Kit. You're over eighteen now." Toddy's expression turned stern. "You don't have any further obligation to the Hansens. Besides, they haven't taken any responsibility for you since you left, have they?"

Kit nodded. "I know. It's just that . . . well, Cora has so much to do, Toddy. There's the cooking and baking and—"

"But you aren't their hired girl! If it wasn't for Miss Cady, you might not even be here! They're not doing a thing to help you earn the money for college, are they?" Toddy's round blue eyes looked serious. "I'll bet they're not even paying you to go out there and work each weekend, are they?"

Once again, Kit shook her head. What Toddy was saying was true, but she felt disloyal to the Hansens for admitting it. After all, they had given her a home and taken care of her when she had no one else. They had fed and clothed her and kept her for almost ten years. Kit couldn't throw these truths away as if they were garbage. Did Kit owe her anything? Probably not, and yet . . . The Hansens weren't perfect but they were all the family Kit had.

She quickly changed the subject. "Speaking of getting paid, I'd better run or I'll be late for work."

Toddy smiled. "I should probably be at the library myself, studying instead of playing tennis. Two more exams to get through. But just think, Kit, the Class of 1900! Isn't it exciting?"

"It sure is." Kit smiled. "I've got to go, Toddy. I'll let you know about Friday."

Kit walked down Main Street under the shade of the elms, thinking about what Toddy had said. If it hadn't been for Miss Cady's encouragement, Kit probably wouldn't have been able to attend high school. This past year, her former teacher had offered Kit a home in Meadowridge so she could finish school and graduate. Kit had readily accepted. She felt sorry for Cora, but Kit knew that if she had remained on the farm she would have been trapped like a rabbit in a cage for the rest of her life.

Thanks to Miss Cady's encouragement, Kit had applied for a scholarship to Merrivale Teachers College. As Kit approached the library, she thought about what a dream come true that would be! Her high school marks were excellent, so all she needed now were her final exam grades. It was a thrilling time to be alive.

Meadowridge Library was an old ivy-covered brick building. Kit hurried through the double oak doors and into the familiar comforting smell of old and new books. Ever since she had discovered it years ago in the third grade, it had been one of her favorite places. She slid her armload of books into the RETURN slot.

"You're late." The head librarian's sharp eyes peered at her over her pinch-nose glasses. "Get to work."

Later that afternoon, Kit was shelving books when Laurel's boyfriend, Dan Brooks, walked through the front door. Kit's hands began to tremble, and she almost dropped the book she was just slipping into its slot.

Dan always had this effect on her. The tall, clean-cut young man often passed her in the hallway at school or on the sidewalk in town, but he only had eyes for Laurel, and Kit knew it. Yet Laurel didn't seem to appreciate how much Dan adored her. Standing in between the shelves among the smells of book glue and paper, Kit silently prayed someday someone would love her too.

On Friday, Miss Cady and Kit arrived at the high school gymnasium, which had been turned into a banquet hall. Long tables had been set up around the room with one T-shaped table in the middle for the principal and teachers. The senior class table extended from the head table and was draped with twisted streamers of green and gold crepe paper. Marking each senior's place was a gold and green satin ribbon with sparkly gold letters reading CLASS OF 1900.

Kit joined Laurel, Chris, Toddy, and Dan at the senior table, then pinned on a ribbon.

When the meal was over, the principal, Mr. Henson, tapped his empty water glass with a fork. "Ladies and gentlemen, tonight we're here to honor several students with special awards for outstanding work, talent, and skill."

On one side of the room, Millicent Cady waited expectantly. The teacher's hands could not keep from fidgeting. Surely Kit would receive the award. Kit was smart and hardworking, disciplined and determined. Millie had helped her fill out the scholarship forms and now the moment of truth was here.

After a few presentations, the principal adjusted his bow tie and collar. "Now we're going to present the scholarship awards. As you know, these are offered to those students with excellent academic standing. Our first one goes to Miss Kathleen Ternan, who has been awarded a full scholarship to Merrivale Teachers College!"

Kit's face went sheet white. It was too good to be true. Her dream was going to become a reality.

On the last regular day of school, the seniors filed into the auditorium for morning assembly. Dressed in a blue suit and striped tie, Mr. Henson stood at the lectern.

"Students, your attention please." The principal waited for the buzzing to die down. "Before you practice for graduation, I want to make an announcement I'm sure you've all been waiting for—this year's salutatorian and valedictorian."

A wave of anticipation rippled across the large hall like a huge wave on the seashore.

The speaker went on. "As you know, these are the two students in the class with the highest grades. The salutatorian makes the welcoming remarks during graduation, and the valedictorian gives the main speech." Mr. Henson fixed the spectacles on his nose as he read. "This year's salutatorian is Daniel Brooks!"

Everyone clapped, especially Kit. Dan was an outstanding student. He deserved the honor. The principal held up his thick hands for silence.

"And now for something special, and I think fitting for the first graduating class of the new century. For the first time in our school's history, this year's valedictorian is a woman—Miss Kathleen Ternan!"

Kit could hear the roars of approval whirling around her. Her heart was beating so hard she was afraid she might explode. The sound of applause was deafening as the entire assembly rose to its feet in a standing ovation.

"Kit! Kit!" Laurel was tugging her arm. "Go up on stage!"

Numb and still not believing the announcement, a shocked Kit made her way up the side steps to the stage. When she reached the center, Mr. Henson shook her hand. Standing beside him, Dan grinned and clapped with the rest. It was the happiest day of Kit's life.

The next day, Kit floated from Miss Cady's cottage to the high school feeling happier and more carefree than she could ever remember. The blue sky promised a perfect day for the class picnic. But even if it had been cloudy, nothing could have spoiled this day for Kit.

Dressed in a crisp, pink-checked gingham dress and straw hat, Kit even felt pretty. The sun's rays bathed her brown hair in gold and gave her skin an apricot glow. At school, her admiring classmates congratulated her, and they laughed together at the countless memories that filled the pages of their yearbook.

Then the senior class went on to the park, where they enjoyed a picnic of cold fried chicken, potato salad, homemade pies and cakes, and of course a freshly sliced watermelon. After lunch, Kit joined Toddy, Laurel, Chris, and Dan for a short walk. The group scaled a rocky hill overlooking the winding ribbon of the river below.

"Written your speech yet, Kit?" Dan teased as they reached the summit.

"Of course! A hundred times, haven't you?" Kit's dark eyes laughed and her pretty white teeth showed through her smile.

"I'm so proud of you both," Toddy chimed in, dancing between the two of them. "Imagine being friends with two celebrities."

The afternoon seemed to stretch endlessly through the day. After a while, Dan and Laurel settled under a shady tree on the crest of the hill, and Chris and Toddy roamed along the path beside the river below. Kit stretched flat on her back and tilted her straw hat over her face.

Insects hummed among the wildflowers nearby. Kit's hands stroked the dry blades of grass that created a scratchy blanket beneath her. A flurry of gnats tried to pester her, but nothing could mar the day. With a wave of her hand, Kit brushed them away. She was going to hold onto this moment forever.

God was truly blessing her. Here she was with her best friends in the world, about to embark on the road to her dream. As a teacher, she could read and write and show others how important learning could be. She would pattern herself after Miss Cady, whose special love extended far beyond the boundaries of the classroom.

For a brief moment as she lay there, Kit found herself missing her Da. Over the years, her feelings of abandonment had lessened. She had been forced to find a way to get through them, but the memory of what had happened to her still hurt.

Her prayer to find Jamie and Gwynny again had not been answered. Where were they? What were they doing now? Kit kept each of her letters tucked away in a cardboard box under her bed, hoping that one day she would be able to deliver them.

But this wasn't a day for sad thoughts. No, this was the kind of day to cherish. Kit wanted to experience every wonderful second of it so she could stash it in the scrapbook of her grateful heart.

"Penny for your thoughts," Dan's voice interrupted her dreaming.

Kit raised herself on her elbows, pushed back the short brim of her straw hat, and smiled at him and Laurel.

"I was thinking about a poem by Elizabeth Barrett Browning about a day like this."

Just then, a shrill whistle pierced the calm air signaling the end of a beautiful day and that they were to gather for the ride back to town.

Kit was the last one to clamber back down the rocky slope. The sun's rays now caressed the hilltops surrounding Meadowridge, sending long purple shadows across the waving blades of grass along the ridge. Only one section of the river shimmered in the light now.

Suddenly, Kit felt strange. She had experienced this feeling before. Her life was going to change—again. Even though it would be a change Kit wanted, she could not escape the feeling she was saying good-bye to something precious. Kit had to accept the fact that her life with these people would never again be quite the same.

7

The day before graduation, Miss Cady was getting ready to leave for her weekly prayer meeting when she found Kit in the kitchen ironing her graduation outfit. The white tucked blouse was simple but dainty, and the white skirt fit Kit's slim figure perfectly.

Miss Cady had suggested that Kit buy a good quality material for the skirt, which she did. And then her teacher had given her a wonderful surprise—real honest-to-goodness lace to trim her blouse! It was delicate and fragile, and it made the blouse like icing finishes a cake. "You'll stand out in your elegant simplicity," Miss Cady had said. "People will see you, not what you're wearing. They'll remember your words, not your dress. And after all, that's the important thing."

Kit wanted to look her very best for the occasion, and as she carefully ironed her new creation, she hoped she would.

Miss Cady had been gone a few minutes when the doorbell rang. Who could that be? Kit wondered as the bell rang again. Quickly she slipped her freshly pressed blouse onto a hanger and hung it on a doorknob before going to answer the door. The bell rang a third time. To her great surprise, it was Cora.

"I almost left. Thought nobody was home," Cora said. "I wuz jest goin' to leave this. But now I see you're here, I'll jest stay and see ya open it." Cora bent down to pick up a large rectangular cardboard box propped beside the front door. "Where's yer bedroom?"

Cora had never visited Miss Cady's cottage before. Somewhat puzzled by this unexpected visit, Kit led the way down the short hallway to her room.

"This doesn't mean you're not coming tomorrow, does it?" Kit asked.

"Oh, no, we're comin' all right." Kit could hear the pride in her voice. "Even Jess, believe it or not. I jest came to brings ya this." Cora laid the box on Kit's bed, then she placed her hands on her hips and pointed. "Well, go ahead. Don't ya want to see what's inside?"

Still baffled, Kit untied the cord around the box and lifted the lid. A huge tidal wave of dismay washed over her.

There in the box under white tissue lay the most awful dress Kit had ever seen. She slowly lifted it out of the box. The sateen dress was blue with white and pink stripes. It had gawdy ribboned sleeves and was trimmed with cheap lace from skirt to bodice.

"Oh, Cora, you shouldn't have."

"I thought you should have a store-bought dress fer once, Kit." The corners of Cora's mouth twitched. The lines in her face creased in an approving smile. "I ordered this out of that mail-order catalog from Chicago. They sell only the latest fashions."

Cora regarded her with satisfaction. She had used her egg money, and she was glad of it. She had stood up to Jess too. He'd wanted Kit to quit at the eighth grade, but his wife wasn't going to let them other orphans in Meadowridge get the upper hand. Nope. Kit was finishing high school and goin' to wear this beautiful bought dress when she did it!

Unable to speak, Kit held the dress up to herself, turning toward the bed so Cora could not see the swell of tears in her eyes.

"You'll have to slip it on with the shoes you'll be wearin' so's we can see if the length is right."

Kit heard Cora's words, but they seemed far away, like the distant squawk of a rooster early in the morning.

"We still have time to take up the hem if needs be."

Kit slipped out of her cotton skirt and shirtwaist and stood in her camisole and petticoat while Cora dropped the dress over her head. Humming quietly under her breath, Cora proceeded to button up the back.

"Well, now, I thinks it's goin' to fit jest fine."

Kit had been a good girl all these years. Cora couldn't have asked for more. Come right down to it, she was glad Kit had come. She would've been hard put to keep things up, especially with her bad back. A sense of longing seeped into her tired aging bones. This would probably be the only high school graduation Cora would ever attend, and she intended to make it the best.

Could Cora hear the loud throbbing in Kit's head? Kit hoped not. Oh, if only the dress would be too small or too tight. Maybe Cora wouldn't be able to button it up, and she wouldn't have to wear it.

"There now. What d'ya think?"

Cora's question pierced Kit's gentle heart as if it were a large darning needle. There was no way out. She would have to wear the dress. In her mind's eye, she could imagine her adoptive mother poring over the pages of the catalog by lamplight. Kit could see her handing one of the boys the order form to fill out because she couldn't read or write. She knew Cora had spent a good deal of time plus her savings on this.

Kit understood what a gift of love this dress was. Just like the time Cora had given Kit the lovely handmade afghan and the time she had stood up to Jess so Kit could keep the kittens. But this was the ultimate test. Kit would have to sacrifice her pride and swallow all her feelings so she wouldn't hurt Cora.

It took Kit only a minute to decide.

"Oh, Cora," she exclaimed with all the enthusiasm she could muster. "Thank you. This was such a thoughtful thing for you to do. I can't tell you how much I appreciate it." She turned around and gave Cora a hug.

"No needs t'make a fuss." Embarrassed, Cora pulled away. "I jest didn't want ya to get up on that platform lookin' dowdy." She took a step back to survey Kit once again. "If I do say so myself, not another girl graduatin' will hold a candle to you in that!"

Then she abruptly turned to leave. "Well, I best be goin' iffen I'm to git home afore dark. I been waitin' and waitin' for this. Don't know how many trips I made to that there postal office."

Kit walked her to the door and watched her climb into the familiar wagon and drive away. Then she shut the door behind her. Why now of all times? Once she would have been thrilled if Cora had bought her a dress from a catalog. But not *now*. Oh, *not* now!

Was this all a bad dream? The material felt sleazy against her skin; the cheap lace scratched her chin and wrists. She collapsed on the sofa. She hated this dress! Kit buried her face in the cushions as bitter tears broke out into hoarse sobs.

As Kit wiped her wet cheeks with the palms of her hands, her eyes caught sight of the freshly pressed white blouse. There it was with its dainty *real* lace still hanging on the doorknob. Kit thought of the hours she had spent sewing it, laboring over its tiny tucks and delicate stitches. She had loved every moment. Now all her effort was wasted.

A while later, Kit heard the front door open and Miss Cady's light steps in the hall.

"Kit, you still up? Do you realize you left the ironing board up and the lamp in the kitchen lit?" She stopped at the half-open bedroom door and saw Kit still wearing the dress. "What on earth are you doing in that?"

Kit straightened up. "Cora brought it to me. It's for graduation."

"To wear?" The teacher's eyebrows spiked up in horror. *"Tomorrow?"*

Kit looked at her sadly. "I don't have a choice, Miss Cady. It's from Cora," she replied with quiet resignation. "I have to."

Moonlight streamed through the lacy curtains of her bedroom, making funny pale shapes on the floor. Kit stood in front of her bedroom mirror tucking tiny white roses into the braided coil of her hair.

She was a blessed young woman to be sure. In spite of the awful dress and her feelings of shame, the gradua- tion ceremony had gone well. The audience had given her speech a long applause, and everyone congratulated her after it was over. Cora had actually hugged her, and for the first time, Kit glimpsed a slight smile on Jess's mouth.

Kit hummed softly. Tonight she would not have to wear the horrid dress. Instead, her simple lace-trimmed blouse and flared white skirt hung on two hangers waiting for her. She slipped into them and twirled around in the bed- room. Tonight was the senior dance, a special night.

The June evening was balmy, and the walk from Miss Cady's cottage to Meadowridge High was short. Toddy and Laurel had already arrived with Chris and Dan. They motioned for her to join them.

The seniors had transformed the school auditorium into a fairyland. Paper Japanese lanterns were strung from the ceiling rafters. A mellow rosy-golden light flooded the room. Already the band was playing a lively tune and couples were dancing.

At once, a group of people clustered around Kit to congratulate her. Just then, the band trumpeted a fanfare.

"Ladies and gentlemen!" the band leader announced across the hall. "The next dance is called the Paul Jones. Ladies, make a circle." He motioned with one hand. "Gentlemen form a circle around them. Now, you'll move counterclockwise to the music, and when it stops, whoever you're standing opposite is your partner for the next set."

"Come on, let's get into the circle!" Toddy grabbed both Laurel and Kit's hands.

The music started, and the two circles began to move. All at once, the band stopped. Kit stood right in front of Dan!

All of a sudden, her secret thoughts about Dan didn't feel quite so secret. Her heart skipped a beat. Kit set her mind to work. After all, Dan had never been interested in any other girl but Laurel. He was a friend, and that is all he would ever be. Laurel was her friend too. A dear friend, just as Toddy was. The three girls were bonded by all the things that had happened to them, what they had survived, and the secrets they shared. She would not do anything to damage her relationship with either of them.

Even as Kit took Dan's hand and let him lead her onto the middle of the dance floor, she mentally put away any fantasies about him. She had her own goals, ambitions, and plans that did not include romance—not at this point in her life. She would finish college, become a teacher like Miss Cady, and maybe some day a writer. But first she was going to try to find Da and her brother and sister.

A few weeks after the dance, Laurel was waiting outside the library when Kit got off work at four o'clock.

"Come over for a visit," she begged, slipping her arm through Kit's as the pair walked down the steps. "I've hardly seen you since graduation, and I need to talk."

Kit hesitated. It bothered her that she could not be as open with Laurel as she had been in the past. A thin screen had been built between them now because of Kit's feelings for Dan. But her friend was very persuasive.

"Please," Laurel pleaded.

"All right," Kit replied.

When they reached the Woodward house, Laurel filled two glasses with fresh lemonade from a pitcher in the icebox. "Papa Lee has taken Mother for a drive in the country," she explained as she pulled several thin molasses cookies from a widemouthed jar on the counter. "We have the whole house to ourselves." She placed the cookies on a plate. "Come on," she instructed, leading the way up the polished stairs to her bedroom.

The pair settled themselves on a window seat overlooking the garden.

Kit looked around appreciatively. She had always admired her friend's lovely room.

"Oh, Kit, I've been absolutely dying to tell this to someone," Laurel exclaimed. "I think I will burst if I don't!"

"What is it?" Kit asked, alarmed.

"My decision," Laurel whispered, looking back at her bedroom door as if someone might walk in at any moment. "I've decided to leave Meadowridge, Kit. I'm going to go to Boston to study voice."

Surprise registered all over Kit's face.

"I know what you're thinking, but Boston is the perfect place. It's where my mother and I lived before she died. My grandmother is there, I'm sure of it, so I'm going to try to find her."

Kit still could not find the words. She looked around the bedroom with its flowered carpet and bookcase stocked with classics, the beautiful ceiling-high armoire filled with Laurel's beautiful clothes. It was obvious that Dr. and Mrs. Woodward cherished Laurel very much.

When her friend didn't say a word, Laurel asked, "Well, what do you think?"

Kit's soft voice grew softer. "What do the Woodwards think, Laurel?"

A shadow crossed Laurel's face. "They don't know yet," she admitted.

Kit's eyebrows lifted, and Laurel rushed on, "I have to go, Kit. I've got to find my family. Surely you understand that. You want to find *your* family! Well, I want to meet my grandmother, somehow. And this is a perfect way."

"But you have so much here," Kit protested. "How can you leave all this?"

"*You're* going away," Laurel accused. "*You're* being true to *yourself,* aren't you?"

"But that's not the same, Laurel. I'm not leaving anything. I'm *going* to something better."

Laurel's dark eyes suddenly had a faraway look in them. "Nothing ever makes up for being an orphan, Kit. Don't you know that?"

Just then the sound of carriage wheels crunching the gravel drifted up through the open bedroom window. The Woodwards' buggy was pulling up next to the doctor's office.

After politely refusing Ava Woodward's invitation for dinner, Kit left. She walked back to the cottage, thinking about what Laurel had confided. Then another thought struck her like a lightning bolt. Laurel hadn't even mentioned Dan! Did he know about her plans? Kit was sure Dan had serious feelings for Laurel. Did this mean Laurel didn't have the same feelings for him?

Poor Dr. and Mrs. Woodward. They would be lost without Laurel. Kit was torn between sympathy for the Woodwards and admiration for her friend who would give up everything to follow her dream. Kit understood. But was it true? Did nothing make up for being an orphan?

9

Summer sped by. Before long, the huge maple trees along the streets of the Arkansas town had started turning gold. Miss Cady's front lawn glistened with light frost each morning. Evenings had turned cool, and the smell of fall was in the air.

Tomorrow Kit would be leaving for Merrivale Teachers College. She still had to pinch herself to believe it, even though she had already received her dormitory room assignment.

In the light of her bedside lamp, she laid five neatly ironed shirtwaists on the top layer of her trunk. Miss Cady had given her a lovely soft knitted coat sweater and matching tam, which she had just packed. These were the last items for now.

Boundless energy seemed to fill her these days. Kit twirled around her bed a few times. When she spotted her leather purse beside the trunk, she opened it and looked inside. It contained the hard-earned money she had saved from her job at the library. And for the twelfth time, she looked at her train ticket. Tomorrow seemed years away.

The sound of loud knocking on the front door interrupted Kit's activity.

Kit heard Miss Cady's voice through her bedroom door. "Why, Lonny Hansen—What on earth brings you all the way into town this late in the evening?"

"Evenin', Miss Cady." Lonny's voice was now the voice of a man. "Is Kit here?"

"Yes, she is—"

By this time, Kit was standing in the hall. She could see Lonny's face. It was ghostly pale.

"What is it, Lonny?" Kit asked.

"Ma's ben took bad, Kit." The young man scrunched the brim of his worn felt hat. "Doc Woodward's out there now. Pa wants to know if you'll come."

"What happened?"

"Some kinda spell. Pa and me found her when we come in from the field. Laid out on the kitchen floor. She cain't talk, Kit. And her face is all twisted. Can you come?"

Miss Cady turned to Kit. "You can't go now. You're leaving tomorrow."

"I got the wagon out front," Lonny's voice quavered. "Pa said to ask you to hurry."

"I'll come, Lonny," Kit replied. "Let me get a few things."

She rushed back to her bedroom. From under her bed, she pulled out her old battered suitcase she had not yet packed.

"Kit, you can't do this!" For the first time Millicent's voice sounded sharp. She now stood in the doorway.

"I have to," was all Kit could say. "Cora's done so much for me."

"Done so much for you?" Miss Cady could hardly believe what was happening. The Hansens had done almost nothing to help Kit. "What have they done? Allowed you to do the chores? Let you sleep in their attic? Come to your senses, Kit!" she pleaded. "You don't owe Cora Hansen a thing."

Kit tossed a few things in the suitcase. "You heard what Lonny said. They need me."

Furious, Miss Cady said, "That old skinflint Jess Hansen should pay somebody to nurse his wife. It's not up to you, Kit. If you go out there, you'll be throwing away everything you've worked for—*we've* worked for! Please, Kit—"

With shaking hands, Kit closed the lid of her suitcase. Why couldn't Miss Cady see how hard this was for her? Kit didn't have a choice. To turn her back on Cora now would be wrong. Kit might not be as strong as an ox, but she was as loyal as the sunrise. This was the right thing to do whether or not Miss Cady understood. Kit had grown up enough to learn that being true to her own heart was one of the most important lessons in life.

"I have to go now, Miss Cady. Lonny's waiting." Kit yanked up the case and grabbed her purse.

"Who knows how long Cora Hansen will live?" Miss Cady demanded. "She may go like *that!*" She snapped her fingers. "Or she might linger for years. You'll be trapped, Kit."

She followed Kit out onto the porch and watched as the slim straight figure got into the waiting wagon. Years of hopes and dreams were suddenly being washed down the drain. *Her* hopes. *Her* dreams that this bright student would go somewhere in life. She began to sob as the wagon pulled away.

Kit had never seen Cora like this. Her gaunt figure lay under a quilt and barely moved. Her face was drawn, and her cheeks were sunken. Her graying hair lay in braids on the pillow, and her eyelids were closed.

"The whole right side is affected," Dr. Woodward told her as soon as she arrived. "She's paralyzed from a stroke. I can't tell how much damage has been done to her brain." The doctor's kind eyes looked at her as he unwrapped the stethoscope from around his neck.

Jess Hansen stood in the doorway, a blank expression on his weathered face. Brown splotches streaked across the chest of his faded denim overalls where he'd wiped his dirty hands. The boys crowded around him.

"She'll need to be turned, moved at least three times a day," the doctor addressed Kit. "Her limbs gently moved and massaged so the muscles don't go bad."

A short while later, Kit watched the doctor's buggy disappear into the dark night. She slumped against the outside front wall.

Her decision to come back had been right. Kit knew that. But now came the hard part—she had to live with the choice. Kit looked up into the sky, speckled with stars. She could not question herself after today. She had to do what must be done and let God take care of the rest.

Help Miss Cady to understand, Lord, she prayed into the night. I would hate to lose her friendship.

A few days later, Kit walked into the kitchen to make some herb tea for Cora. She discovered Jess Hansen sitting at his usual place, holding a knife and fork in both fists.

"When's supper?" he demanded, almost in a snarl.

Kit stopped in her tracks. The old feelings of fear almost strangled her. Instantly, she knew what she had to do.

"I didn't come here to be your hired help, Jess." This time, Kit didn't need Cora. She could stand up to him on her own. "I'm here to look after Cora. She's my only duty. I suggest that if you and the boys want to eat, you either fix it yourselves or hire a cook."

A short while later, while sitting at Cora's side, Kit heard the rattle of pots and pans. Jess and the boys were fixing their own supper. Kit had conquered her fear of Jess Hansen at last. She was growing up.

Little by little, Cora Hansen began to recover from her stroke. Kit massaged her limbs and exercised them daily. She also fed her and read her stories to pass the time. Gradually, the ailing woman was able to sit up in her bedroom chair, and her speech began to come back too. By the summer of 1902, Lonny Hansen had found someone else to help, and Kit felt free to leave.

About this time, Miss Smedley, the Meadowridge librarian, informed Kit that the town's newspaper was looking for a reporter. Kit decided to apply.

At the office of the *Meadowridge Monitor,* Kit timidly pushed open the door. Instantly, a mixture of smells met her: printer's ink, fresh paper, machinery oil. A lady sporting Ben Franklin glasses waited on customers at the high counter up front.

"I'm here to apply for the job," Kit said to the woman at the counter. She had a strong reference from the high school principal and felt confident.

"See Mr. Clooney, the editor." The woman pointed to a little man hunched over a cluttered rolltop desk to the side. All Kit could see of his face was the green eyeshade wrapped around the front of his bald head.

"Never had a woman reporter," Ed Clooney grumbled a few minutes later after he had read the principal's recommendation. "I guess we can give it a try though. When can you start?"

"Right away!" Kit exclaimed.

In August, she rented Miss Cady's quaint little house, only this time Kit lived alone with Ginger, her tabby cat. Miss Cady had taken a teaching position in another town and had just moved away. Before she left, however, she and Kit had time to mend their relationship. Over time, her mentor had recovered from her disappointment and had accepted Kit's decision. Kit was glad her relationship with her beloved teacher had been restored.

Kit looked forward to each day. She felt so alive and so happy. She loved everything about working at the newspaper: the sound of the big press rolling on Thursdays, the smell of the fresh paper and the printer's ink, the rustle of the newspapers as they were being stacked for sale.

Her first reporting assignments were small ones. She picked up ad copy from various Meadowridge stores and brought them to Mr. Clooney to rewrite or lay out for printing. Eventually, however, Kit began to cover town meetings and interview special officials. As time went on, she found fewer penciled changes on her stories.

As she wrote articles for the newspaper, she also wrote letters to her lost brother and sister and Da, something she had continued to do over the years. Somehow these letters anchored Kit's life. She could let her feelings flow freely through her words. The letters had become a story—her personal journey.

Late one afternoon after work, Kit untied her laced shoes and tucked her stocking feet under her legs. On the table beside the sofa, Ginger licked his furry stripes in the warmth of the sun. Kit petted him before pulling her writing pad out of the drawer.

It's October now in Meadowridge. I love to walk through the fallen leaves along Main Street as I go to work each morning, hearing them crunch under my feet. Wood smoke mixed with the smell of newly mown hay drifts in from the fields nearby and reminds me of the Hansens. Cora is much better. She seems very glad to see me each time I visit. The boys are working hard with Jess, getting the fields ready for winter. I'm glad to be here. This little house gives me a sense of belonging. And yet, somehow I feel restless, melancholy, like hearing a train whistle at night and wondering where the train is going. I feel like I should be on it. Maybe one day I will be.

11

The days of October slipped into November 1902. On Thanksgiving Day, Kit attended the special service at the Meadowridge Community Church. The November sunshine slanted through the church windows onto the golden wheat decorating the front of the altar. As she slipped into her pew, she remembered last year.

Had it already been a year since Laurel's marriage to Gene Michela? Kit had liked the Italian singer from Boston very much and was thrilled that things had worked out so well for her dear friend. She and Laurel missed Toddy, though, who was now attending nursing school. Mrs. Hale told Kit that Toddy would be home sometime next year, however, for the library dedication to Helene.

Following the service, people turned to greet one another with smiles and wishes for the holiday. It was then that Kit felt a touch on her shoulder. She turned to see Dan Brooks!

"Dan! What a surprise!" she exclaimed. "What are you doing here?"

He smiled. "I'm spending Thanksgiving with my grandmother and aunts, but I'm actually on my way to San Francisco."

"San Francisco?"

"Yes, I've been accepted as an intern at a hospital there. I start next week. Decided to stop in Meadowridge for a short visit." He paused. "It's good to see you, Kit. Would you like to have a cup of coffee?"

A warm feeling of pleasure poured over her. "I'd love to," she replied shyly.

The fallen leaves that cluttered the sidewalk crunched under their feet as they walked up Front Street toward the Meadowridge Inn. The day was clear but chilly.

"It's great to see you, Kit," Dan said. "I wasn't sure any of the old crowd would be around."

Kit smiled. Dan noticed her complexion was now tinged with pink.

"So, do you still want to be a writer?" he asked as a horse and buggy clopped by.

"I *am* a writer, Dan! And I get paid for it," she laughed. "I'm a reporter for the *Monitor*."

Dan nodded his dark curly head. "I remember Miss Cady telling us back in grammar school that you had real talent. She was right, you know."

By this time, they had reached the inn. Dan put his hand on Kit's elbow as they mounted the stone steps. Once a stagecoach stop, the rambling clapboard building had a rustic charm. Inside it was a fine modern hotel.

The head waiter escorted the pair to a sunny corner overlooking the town park. The weeping willows were in plain view. Two dogs were sniffing out tunnels through the dried leaves.

"I guess you knew—" Kit began.

"I just heard—" Dan started in.

They both laughed.

He circled his coffee mug with a finger. "I know about Laurel," he said. "My grandmother told me."

Kit felt the old twinge as she saw Dan's square jaw tighten. He's still in love with Laurel, she thought. Sympathy overrode her own longing. She reached over and patted his hand.

"You know, Dan, she had to go back to Boston. She was never really satisfied here."

Dan nodded. "Things have sure changed in the last three years." He poured a heaping spoonful of sugar into his steaming coffee.

"Are you surprised?"

Suddenly, Dan's dark eyes regarded her intently.

"*You* haven't changed. Have you?"

"Nothing ever stays the same, Dan. Not even me." She fingered the edge of her coffee cup. "For instance, I don't know how long I'll stay at the *Monitor*."

Dan was startled by her reply. He looked at her again. Why hadn't he noticed before how pretty she was?

"You *should* think about it. There's a whole big world out there with lots of newspapers. You could get a job anywhere."

"I intend to!" Kit's words surprised her as much as anyone. She had never shared this secret longing with anyone. Now she was actually telling Dan!

The two young people talked for a long time.

"We'd better get going," Kit finally announced. "My editor is a widower, and he's planning a Thanksgiving dinner for all of us on staff. I promised a salad."

Dan looked disappointed. "I was hoping you might come home and have dinner with us."

"Thank you, but no. I've promised them."

Outside on the wide front porch, they said their good-byes.

"It's been wonderful seeing you again, Dan." Kit held out her gloved hand. "I hope it won't be so long before the next time." She turned up her coat collar as she hurried down the steps.

"Take care, Kit!"

At the corner, Kit turned around for one last look. Dan was still standing where she had left him. She lifted her hand and waved.

12

January 1905

Kit stood next to her editor's jumbled rolltop desk. He was staring silently out the front plate glass window toward the town square. It was a dreary winter day. Silvery sheets of rain streaked down the front windowpanes. Mr. Clooney's ancient chair squeaked as he swiveled around.

"Well, if you've made up your mind to go, Kit, I can't stop you." He began arranging piles of scattered notes. "San Francisco is a far piece, you know. And you're not going to find it easy on a big city paper." The editor shook his head in disapproval. "Some editors still don't accept lady newspaper writers. But you're a fine reporter. You can do it.

"I suppose you want a recommendation from me?" he said pretending to be irritated. "That's asking a lot, I'd say. Give you a good send-off to another newspaper when I'm losing the best reporter I've ever had." He pushed his green visor back from his brow.

Kit smiled. "Thank you, Mr. Clooney."

The last two weeks before Kit left for San Francisco were busy ones. Kit started packing boxes and saying her good-byes. She made one last trip out to the Hansen farm to see Cora and leave her cat, Ginger.

On a cold February afternoon, she borrowed Mr. Clooney's buggy and mare. When she reached the front drive, a group of scrawny chickens fluttered out of the buggy's way. The barn door was latched, and the old clothesline was empty. It was too cold for laundry today.

"Oh, Kit, come in." Lonny's wife held a rosy-cheeked baby on her hip. "Cora will be so pleased to see you."

The fragrance of cinnamon scented the air. Starched blue curtains at the front windows and a bright cross-stitched tablecloth gave the room a cheerful look. An arrangement of dried flowers adorned the pine hutch.

"Everything looks so nice, Alverna," Kit commented, as Ginger jumped out of her arms to dart up the narrow stairs. "Thanks for taking my cat for me." Kit's sadness at leaving her beloved cat remained hidden in her heart. "I knew he'd be most at home here. I hope I'll be able to get him one day."

"You're welcome, Kit," the younger woman replied as they walked down the hall. "He'll be fine." She pushed open the bedroom door. "Ma, you've got company."

Cora was sitting in the old rocker by the window, a multicolored handmade quilt draped over her lap. She slowly turned her head. Kit was shocked to see how much she had aged. Although she had improved for a while, the doctor had warned them the paralysis would have a long-term effect. Her thin body looked like a skeleton with clothes on. Her hair had turned completely white.

And now it was almost impossible to understand her garbled words.

Kit pulled up a straight-backed chair. She took Cora's wrinkled hand in hers.

"Cora, I'm going away," she began. "I have a job with a newspaper in San Francisco, California. I'll be leaving Meadowridge next week." When the invalid nodded her head, Kit knew she understood.

A few minutes later, Alverna appeared with a tray of tea and freshly baked gingersnaps. "Thought you ladies would enjoy a little refreshment," she said cheerfully as she set the tray on the dresser.

Cora mumbled something Kit couldn't understand.

"Yes, Ma, I'll show her," the younger woman replied.

Alverna walked over to a shelf and pulled off a thick bound book. She laid it on Kit's lap. "Open it," she instructed.

To Kit's amazement, the book turned out to be a scrapbook with all of her newspaper articles pasted on page after page. Kit could hardly believe it. Cora had been keeping a copy of everything Kit had ever published!

All at once, the haggard woman slumped in her chair.

"I think Ma's tired, Kit," Alverna whispered.

Kit cradled the scrapbook under one arm as she leaned over to kiss Cora's cheek. "I have to leave now, Cora. Take care of yourself. I'll see you when I come back to Meadowridge." Kit thought she saw a tear trickle down the old woman's wrinkled cheek.

"Ma's been keepin' everythin' you've written, Kit," Alverna told her as Kit handed her the book. They walked toward the front door. "Even though she don't read, she recognizes your name, Kathleen Ternan."

Kit's heart was filled with memories and nostalgia as she rode back to town. She only hoped she had made Cora's life better. After all was said and done, Kit knew that she was a better person for having known Cora Hansen.

San Francisco

From the books she had read, Kit imagined California to be a land of sunshine, orange groves, and tropical
palms. She was shocked to discover that San Francisco
could be overcast with gray skies and a sharp salty wind.
The day she arrived, a fog also hovered over the city.

At the train station, Kit hired a cabby to take her to
the *San Francisco Times* to check in. Near the end of the
day, after hours of trudging up and down hills, Kit finally
found a room to rent. It was in a three-story frame house
on Market Street.

The door was opened by a sallow-faced woman with
gray hair pulled back into a tight bun who eyed her sus-
piciously. "I require a month's rent in advance," she said
as she led Kit upstairs.

On the second floor, the landlady opened the door to
room number 4. "Most people like a front room. This one
rents for six dollars a week, but I rent by the month
'cause I don't like people comin' and goin'. And I don't
give refunds," the woman said.

Kit walked to the center of the room. It had a brass bed, a washstand with a pitcher and bowl, a bureau with a mirror, and a table by a bay window.

"Bathroom's down the hall. You sign up for baths. Number 4 gets Tuesdays and Fridays."

Suddenly, Kit felt exhausted. The weeklong train trip, the hectic changes in St. Louis and Chicago, and the busyness since her arrival had all taken a toll on her.

"I'll take it," she said, opening her purse to take out the month's rent.

The landlady counted the bills. "Well, that's it then." She turned to go, then said, "By the way, I'm Mrs. Bredesen."

At the window, Kit drew aside the stiff net curtains. The sun was peeking from behind a ceiling of low clouds. The clanging of the horse-drawn streetcars, the smell of fish from the Bay, the tall buildings—how different this was from Meadowridge!

Built on more than forty hills, San Francisco was alive with activity. From her place on top of one of the hills, Kit could see fishing boats sailing back into the Bay to unload their catch. She spotted red cable cars that looked like toys running along rails up and down the steep streets. People hurried everywhere. Some wore blue cotton coats and trousers and carried baskets of vegetables on poles. Kit knew these were the Chinese. Some were walking around in black frock coats. Kit assumed they were business people. Kit even thought she spotted a few miners, dressed in flannel shirts and boots. The city was home to many other nationalities too, such as Italians and Germans.

A brisk knock interrupted her window sight-seeing tour.

"Here's your linen." Mrs. Bredesen reappeared with an armload of white sheets and striped towels. "You get clean linen once a week, towels twice. There's a laundry chute at the end of the hall."

"Thank you," Kit murmured, taking the pile from her.

"One more thing." The landlady pointed to a white card tacked to the back of the apartment door. "These here are the rules: No cooking, no entertaining guests of the opposite sex, no staying out past 11:00 P.M."

Kit nodded.

"Well, I guess that's all," the landlady concluded. "You want meals? They're extra. Will cost ya fifty cents a week if ya want coffee and rolls in the mornin'."

"I'll let you know."

Kit locked the door behind her, took off her laced shoes, and wiggled her tired feet. At least she had a place to live. Suddenly a wave of loneliness swept over her. She was more alone than she had ever been. She didn't know a soul in San Francisco.

After unpacking a few things and making her bed, she emptied the contents of her purse on the bed. Dan's scribbled address fell out. She'd almost forgotten. Somewhere in this strange big city she *did* know someone. Dan! He was completing his medical degree here, and his mother had asked her to look him up. Said he was working so hard he didn't have time to make friends.

Kit tucked the small square of pink paper in a side pocket and opened her money compartment. The trip to California had been costly, and the food had been expensive. Kit counted what was left. A small alarm bell clanged in her head, but she refused to listen to it. In just two weeks she would collect her first paycheck. Things would work out. "All things work together for good to them that love God," she reminded herself.

Slowly, Kit sank onto the bed and curled up on top of Cora's afghan. She leaned back against the bed pillows. Before she knew it she had drifted off into some much needed sleep.

Life at the newspaper was packed with excitement. Kit's boss, Clem Stoniger, a veteran reporter with a wealth of newspaper experience, took the young reporter under his wing.

Kit's early duties were routine tasks such as checking accident reports and writing obituaries. "Your time will come," the white-haired man said as he leaned back in his chair. "Sometimes it's just being in the right place at the right time. You never know when you'll get your chance to report the BIG story." His kind hazel eyes smiled at her.

Kit hoped he was right. She tried to record her impressions and descriptions of the people and incidents she observed. It was all part of becoming a writer. Many times at night she wrote in her journal. Letters to her father and brother and sister poured out of her.

Dear Da and Jamie and Gwynny,

I've been in San Francisco three months now, and I am growing to love it. I've even made a friend. Her name is Nelly Armstrong. She takes classified ads at the *Times*. Nelly is fun-loving and carefree, and we have been able to spend some of our days off together. I'm trying to learn as much about the city as I can. Like a pocketful of different coins, the city has many faces. I live on Market Street. It has street vendors and small shops. Expensive shops line Montgomery Street. And on Nob Hill, the homes look like palaces. San Francisco has a big opera house too. Many folks at the *Times* have gone. They tell me the music is beyond imagining. I still miss you all, and I pray that one day we will meet again.

Your daughter and sister forever,
Kit

On Kit's days off, she liked to wander down to Fisherman's Wharf to watch the fishing boats come in. Her new friend, Nelly, frequently joined her since they lived only a few blocks apart. The men at the Wharf worked in rhythm like the drum section of a band. Many were Italian and often could be heard singing and talking in their native language.

One week, Kit wrote a human interest story about a miner. He was seventy if he was a day. Even though the old codger had lost several fortunes panning for gold, he was convinced he could find the "Lost Dutchman" mine. Kit's story covered the man's hopes and dreams.

"You're getting there." Mr. Stoniger ripped a typed sheet of paper from his typewriter. "You've the makings of a feature writer, Kit. Remember," he said as he slipped a clean sheet into the carriage, "one rule of good writing is to rewrite. Always answer these five questions: who? what? when? where? and why? The key is to check your facts and write from the heart."

In her letters to Mr. Clooney at the *Monitor,* Kit described many of the sights and sounds of the city. Her former editor enjoyed them so much he asked her to write a regular feature for the paper: "City Sights and Insights" by Kathleen Ternan. She was thrilled that her work was being published in two newspapers!

One morning, Kit was finishing a story for the afternoon run. Notes, clippings, and paper fastened with paper clips were spread across her desk. All of a sudden, a strong hand clamped her left shoulder.

"Hi, Kit!"

She recognized Dan's voice instantly.

"Dan!" she exclaimed, nearly jumping out of her chair. "What a surprise!"

Dan seemed taller and better looking than ever.

"How in the world did—"

Dan cut in. "My aunt cut one of your columns out of the *Monitor* and mailed it to me. I decided to look you up."

The clicking of typewriters and noise in the newsroom surrounded them. Dan glanced around. Offices with window shades open and closed lined the large room. Men in shirt sleeves with pencils tucked behind their ears were in constant motion. Cigar smoke clogged the air. Piles of newspapers bound with string were stacked in the corners.

"This certainly is a busy place!" Dan said. "Almost makes the hospital look dull."

"I doubt that," Kit laughed.

"Well, I know you're working." Dan looked at the half-finished copy on her desk. "My next day off from the hospital is Wednesday. I was wondering if we might get together."

Kit sighed. "I can't, Dan. I'm not off until Thursday. I'm supposed to cover the mayor's speech on Wednesday."

"Well, I'll just have to switch days then." He smiled. "Thursday it is. I'll stop by to get you. Where do you live?"

Kit quickly scratched her Market Street address on a scrap piece of paper lying nearby and handed it to Dan.

"Great." He folded it and put it in his vest pocket. "About ten?"

Kit nodded.

Dan practically skipped down the stairs. It was good to see Kit. He wished he'd known she was here earlier, but he'd been working such long hours, he barely even knew San Francisco! Oh, well, maybe now he would get the chance to see more of it. No, maybe now he would *take* the chance to see more of it.

Kit was thinking much the same as Dan. It was so good to see him again. She guessed they both needed a familiar face. Kit tried to get back to work on the article she'd been writing before Dan's unexpected visit. She had an article to finish and pronto!

Dressed in the blue suit Mrs. Woodward had given her before she left Meadowridge, Kit was ready when Dan arrived a few minutes earlier than planned. The pair immediately set off down Market Street.

"I've been so cooped up in the hospital that I feel like I've been let out of prison," he explained as they trudged down the long steep hill. "The schedule for residents is backbreaking."

"You haven't changed your mind about wanting to be a doctor, have you?"

"Oh, no," he replied. "But I'm looking forward to becoming a country doctor."

Kit glanced at him with question marks in her eyes.

"Didn't I tell you? Before I started medical school, Dr. Woodward promised me that when I finish, I can go back to Meadowridge and practice with him."

For a moment, Kit's heart sank. This meant Dan would be leaving San Francisco at the end of his residency. And the two of them had just reconnected!

She tried to shake her disappointment. "No, you hadn't told me. But of course this is the first time we've seen each other since that Thanksgiving Day."

"That's right, Kit. And I've thought a lot about that day we spent together."

They finally reached the bottom of the hill.

"You know, it's strange that we both ended up in San Francisco," Dan said. "It's so far from Meadowridge."

A sharp wind off the Bay sent whitecaps dancing across the dark blue water. Rows of open crates packed with salmon and shrimp and halibut on ice formed an open-air market along Fisherman's Wharf. The couple joined the throng of buyers, sniffing the fishy air and enduring the salty spray.

For lunch, the two friends went to Chinatown. Dan insisted on eating with chopsticks, but Kit just couldn't manage them and requested a fork. Afterward, they wandered through the colorful shops, enjoying the delicate figurines, carved ivory, and beautiful teakwood screens.

Early that evening as the gas streetlights came on, Dan suggested they have dinner at a nearby French restaurant one of his medical professors had told him about.

"But Dan." Knowing a medical resident's small salary, Kit protested, "Those restaurants are pretty expensive."

Dan whipped out his wallet and a crisp new fifty-dollar bill. "Don't worry, this is on Uncle Ned. He sent me this in a letter and told me to find a pretty girl and take her out on the town." Dan flipped the wallet closed and slipped it into his back pocket. "So, I've found the pretty girl. Now, shall we go?"

On the way, Dan told her how generous his uncle had been to him through college and the lean years of interning and residency. "If it hadn't been for Uncle Ned," he shrugged his broad shoulders, "I wouldn't have made it."

By a window overlooking the Bay, the couple sat down at a white-linen-covered table with a bud vase in the middle that held a red rose. Kit's eyes opened as wide as saucers when the waiter handed her the menu: deviled crabs a la Creole, roast lamb with mint sauce, and filet of beef with bordelaise sauce for the main dishes. Lemon ice cream and strawberry bavaroise for dessert. Kit hardly knew where to begin. Throughout dinner, the couple talked and shared.

"Kit, I can't remember when I've had such a good time." They had reached Kit's door, and Dan's warm grip was strong but gentle as he squeezed both of Kit's hands. "Thanks!"

"Thank you, Dan," she replied. "And thank your Uncle Ned!"

"How about your next day off?" he asked.

Kit could hardly believe it. The day had seemed like a wonderful dream, and now he was inviting her for another.

"Fine," she managed to say. Then he gave her a smile and dashed down the stairs hurrying to catch the last trolley back to the hospital.

Over the next few months, Dan and Kit explored San Francisco as if it were a gold mine. They walked on the beach, took a ferry across the Bay, packed picnic lunches to eat in the park, and sampled fried fantail shrimp at the wharf. They even began choosing a few restaurants to call their own.

During this time, Kit shared her hopes and dreams about becoming a writer.

"I'm very grateful to Mr. Clooney, who gave me my start," she told Dan one chilly evening as they sipped coffee at a favorite restaurant. "And Clem Stoniger keeps telling me my big chance will come." Tiny chocolate shavings dimpled the whipped cream dollop on the top of her coffee. "I hope it comes soon!"

"I know what you mean," Dan replied, stirring his coffee. "I'm looking forward to practicing in Meadowridge. I keep telling myself the chance will be here before I know it."

Kit's feelings for Dan were becoming stronger. Dan was a good friend, but she knew in her heart he had always been more. The past few weeks had been so wonderful, and Kit's heart had been soaring. Yet, she felt like San Francisco was the place she was supposed to be. She wasn't going back to Meadowridge. Refusing to let her emotions ruin the evening, she stashed her feelings in the bottom drawer of her mind, hoping she could ignore them.

16

Kit turned in her day's copy. Sweeping all her notes and clippings and pencils into the drawer, she shoved it closed and locked it. Then she threw the long straps of her bag over her shoulder.

"Good-bye, Nelly!" she called out as she passed the classified ad desk on her way out.

"Have a good time!" Nelly smiled as her friend dashed out the revolving doors and into the April sunshine.

Spring had come suddenly to San Francisco. Kit felt the warmth of the sun on her back as she strolled along. Keeping the smile off her face was as hard as washing freckles off a child's nose. Every time she tried, it would creep back on. Tonight, she and Dan were actually going to attend the opening performance of Bizet's *Carmen* starring the famous Enrico Caruso at the San Francisco Opera House. The entertainment editor of the *Times* had given her free tickets.

This afternoon everyone Kit passed seemed happy too. Maybe it was the weather. Maybe it was the colorful displays in the store windows she passed. Maybe it was the vendor's carts overflowing with spring flowers on the street corners. Kit didn't know, but she did know that today she felt as light and carefree as a birthday balloon.

All of a sudden, she stopped short. There in the window of a milliner's shop was the most beautiful hat she had ever seen. Fashioned of soft pale blue straw, the crown was wrapped with lavender satin ribbon. Nestled in the brim was a cluster of deep purple silk violets.

Kit's fingers tightened around her handbag. Inside was her week's paycheck. Mentally she ticked off the bills she had to pay. Yet, when would another evening like this pass her way? Surely such an event deserved something special to wear. And after all, she'd been working at the *Times* more than a year now without buying anything special.

Impulsively, she opened the shop door and went inside. Twenty minutes later, a round hatbox containing layers of thin tissue paper and one elegant blue hat emerged with its proud owner. It was a reckless purchase, but this would be a night to remember.

Now that her paycheck had been cashed, Kit felt even more carefree. She bought herself a pair of lavender gloves and a matching scarf made with real Belgian lace to drape around the collar of her good gray suit. By the time she had finished shopping, she also owned a bar of creamy scented soap and a small bottle of cologne. Kit's happiness shone on her face.

That evening, the opera hall glittered. Ladies dressed in elegant gowns and jewels, their gentlemen escorts in splendid evening clothes, mingled about. Sitting with Dan, Kit observed every detail. The opera house had tiers of balconies down to the main floor with a sweeping staircase leading up to them. As the overture rose from the orchestra pit, the heavy red velvet curtain lifted and the performance began. The whole evening was unforgettable.

After the performance, the couple dined on creamy pasta and crusty sourdough bread at one of their favorite small restaurants along North Beach. It was almost midnight when Dan walked Kit up Market Street to her boardinghouse in the light of the street lamps. He took Kit's gloved hand in his.

"You know, Kit," he said, "you've introduced me to so many experiences I would've missed these past few months. I had a wonderful evening."

The city was quiet now. Only a few clangs and rambles of passing trolley cars broke the late night stillness. At the front steps to Kit's boardinghouse, the couple stopped.

"Thanks for one of the greatest evenings of my life," Dan said softly before leaning over and kissing Kit lightly. Then he teased, "Oh, I meant to tell you," he added, "that's the dandiest hat I've ever seen!"

Kit watched as he went whistling down the hill. She tiptoed up to her room. It was early morning now. Her landlady would complain, but Kit didn't care. It had been worth it. Once inside her room, she halted in front of the mirror and tilted her head from one side to the other. It *was* a beautiful hat. Ever so carefully, she lifted it off and set it on the bureau where she could see it from the bed.

Humming the aria from *Carmen,* Kit waltzed around the room, spinning and spinning. It was a date she would always remember—April 17, 1906.

17

It was 5:13 on the morning of April 18. Snuggled under her warm striped afghan, a contented Kit slept peacefully. She didn't know the pebbles on the cobblestone streets around the city were beginning to vibrate. She had no idea that the spikes on the rail tracks were starting to ping.

Then without warning, a violent movement startled her. Kit bolted upright. Her brass bed was rocking to and fro as if a giant fist were shaking it. Kit held on to both sides of the mattress. The sound of dogs yelping frantically was drowned out by a hissing sound from somewhere. All at once, the creaking and cracking and splitting sounds surrounded her. She opened her mouth to scream, but nothing came out.

Suddenly, the bedroom window shattered into a million pieces, and her mirror crashed to the floor. Her bureau pitched forward, dumping clothes everywhere. Her earthenware pitcher and washbowl slid off the washstand. The building moaned and groaned. The walls shook and trembled so much that Kit was afraid they might collapse on top of her. The floor swelled up and down, rocking the bed like a storm-tossed ship.

The roar was deafening. Kit wanted to cover her ears with her hands, but she didn't dare let go. The sound seemed to go on forever. Then, with one final jolt, the walls shuddered and everything quivered to a halt.

Kit could hear nothing.

For what seemed an eternity, she huddled in her covers, shivering and waiting for what might be next. Nothing. Dead silence. Finally, she swung her legs over the side of the bed, now up against a wall. The floor tilted like a ride at the fair, so Kit gingerly tested her weight.

Whatever had happened, she knew she had to get out of the building. It might topple at any moment. She crept over to the open space that once was the window. In the predawn light, she could see people pouring out of the buildings on both sides of Market Street. "Earthquake! Earthquake!"

Within moments, Kit heard voices and rushing feet outside in the hall. Dashing to the door, she tugged at the doorknob frantically. The door wouldn't budge; it was twisted in the door frame. Kit darted to the window. Could she possibly climb out onto the roof and slide down to the ledge above the front porch?

Quickly, she grabbed her skirt and blouse and somehow got them on. With her shoes tied by their laces around her neck and her notebook stuffed into her handbag, she started out the window. The ground was a long way away. Feeling dizzy, she gripped the windowsill to steady herself. Her heart was beating like a bass drum, but she knew she had to get out or be trapped in the house if another quake hit. The aftershocks were sometimes worse than the earthquakes themselves.

"Dear God, help me," she prayed.

A quiet voice bubbled up from somewhere deep within her soul: *Fear thou not; for I am with thee: be not dismayed; for I am thy God.* It was a verse she had learned many years ago in Sunday school. The beating of her heart settled into a steady rhythm. Somehow everything would be all right. God was still in control. In spite of the way she felt, he had not left.

Perched on the sill, Kit cast a last look at her room and saw her beautiful blue straw hat! It had tumbled to the floor, but it was still in one piece. Hesitating only a split second, she jumped back into the room to grab it and jammed it on her head.

Cautiously, she crawled to the edge of the roof with the straps of her handbag slung over one shoulder and her shoes still hanging around her neck.

"Wait a minute, lady!" a male voice screamed from the front sidewalk below. "Don't try to climb down by yourself!"

The fog was as thick as smoke. Kit peered over the ledge. She could just make out the form of someone below.

"It's a pretty good drop." The stranger cupped his hands and yelled. "Try to lower yourself slowly, and I'll catch you."

From the second story, the shadowy man looked big enough. Kit would have to trust how strong he was. She prayed, lowered herself over the gutter, and let go. As she fell, a shoe smacked her in the mouth. She screamed just as she pummeled the man to the ground. Her fall sent them both sprawling onto the dewy grass.

"Thank you!"

The stranger jumped up and then stuck a rugged hand out to help her. "You're welcome," he replied, catching his breath.

All at once, Kit's mind began racing. Here she was in the middle of an earthquake! She had heard about earthquakes before but had never experienced one. From what she could see of her own dilapidated building, this one had created a disaster. Kit was at the right place at the right time! Mr. Stoniger had told her to watch for it.

Barefoot and chilly, Kit dug into her handbag for her notebook and pencil. "Sir?" she asked. "May I have your name?"

Even as she scribbled the man's own earthquake story, her mind was racing. This was it! The BIG one! Kit knew it, and she was right here in it. This was her big chance. The story of the century.

Kit plunked down on the broken steps to her apartment building. People were wandering around in a state of bewilderment, not knowing where they were going. Kit could hear the sobbing of a child across the street. Draped in a tattered burgundy bathrobe with her hair in curlers, Mrs. Bredesen sat to one side. Her eyes were dazed. She didn't look at Kit or say a word. She just sat there. Moving like two wooden puppets, an older couple walked arm in arm through the debris. Kit quickly tied her shoes and swept up her hair with a few hairpins from the bottom of her purse.

As the heavy fog lifted over San Francisco, messages began to filter in from other parts of the city. The people received word that entire blocks of houses had collapsed, trapping their occupants in the wreckage. Some streets were so badly split that boards had to be laid over their cracks.

Slowly, people from other parts of the city arrived. Some were barefoot but wearing street clothes over their nightgowns and carrying what was left of their belongings. They asked about relatives. They asked about neighbors. They asked about a place to stay.

Kit wondered about the newspaper building. What had happened to the huge press machines and the shelves of lead type? Had her cubicle and the main office survived? Kit determined she would plod on with her story no matter what had happened to the *Times*. She'd worry about that later.

Military personnel on horseback came from the Golden Gate Fort. Armed with rifles and megaphones, they ordered, "Do not go back inside! The buildings aren't safe. If you need shelter, we'll escort you to the fort. There is a place to stay there. Any medical personnel must report to the military compound at once. We need all doctors and nurses. Please!"

What about Dan? Had he survived? Kit had already heard that the big downtown hospital had been hit hard. Rescue parties were trying to find and bring out those who had been injured or trapped in the wreckage. If Dan had survived, Kit knew he would be trying to help others, with no thought for his own safety.

As evening came, Kit noticed a strange red glow in the eastern sky. With pencil in hand, she stopped writing. Horrified, she saw a black cloud had enveloped an entire section of the city below. Was it a storm cloud? No, it was a fire! Fire! Monstrous flames filled the sky. Orange and gold and yellow blazed. Flames leaped between the buildings. Everyone on the hilltop around her watched in silent horror. The fire was devouring section after section. Water pumped from the Bay failed to quench its great thirst.

Smoke was dense. The smell of burning wood and scorched straw overwhelmed the onlookers. Explosions resounded across the city. Over and over, one right after the other. Panic gripped each soul as the buildings blew up and caved in before their very eyes.

"The gas mains have broken!" one desperate onlooker cried.

"But where are the firefighters? What's happened?"

It was only days later that Kit learned the city's main water pipes had crossed directly over the path of the San Andreas Fault. The raging inferno had devoured the city, house by house, street by street. Because of the damage done to the water pipes by the quake, there had been nothing to stop the ravenous fire except time.

By nightfall, fog had rolled in from the Bay and joined the cloud of smoke, swallowing the entire city. Foghorns wailed their call in the distance. An eerie silence hung over the city.

18

Here and there, clusters of people settled down along Market Street to spend the night. Most of them had no food because they had fled their houses in panic. Slowly, small campfires were lit, inviting friend and stranger alike to gather around for warmth. Still in her robe and curlers, Mrs. Bredesen hovered around one nearby. While the disaster had broken up buildings and homes, it was building a spirit of unity.

Her pencil worn to a nub, an exhausted Kit yanked her hat off and plopped down on a stoop. So much of what she had seen and experienced this day had seemed unreal. There was too much to make sense of it all.

The idea for the beginning of her story began to take shape. She flipped open her pad and began writing furiously in the dimming light.

The Ferry Building at the foot of Market Street remained gleaming white among charred telephone poles, cracked cement, and piles of rubble, the hands of the clock on its side eerily stopped at exactly 5:13 A.M., the time the earthquake struck.

That night, police and military soldiers patrolled the streets. When they reached the top of Market Street, they alerted the citizens that looters would be shot on sight.

Hundreds of people who had not gone to the fort now followed the horseback riders to Golden Gate Park, where canvas tents had been set up as temporary shelters for the homeless.

"Miss, do you have a place to stay?" The policeman's voice was kind.

"I don't know," Kit said. "My building isn't safe and—"

"Kit! Kit! Is that you?"

At that moment, Kit heard a familiar voice through the dark. A woman was running toward her waving an arm in the air. It was Nelly!

"Oh, Nelly," Kit cried as they embraced. "I'm so glad to see you!"

"Me too," her friend replied. "It's been a long day."

Kit soon learned that the newspaper building had been destroyed. Messages were being sent off the postal wire, and reporters were filing their stories from Oakland. Nelly also related that her own one-story house was still standing.

"I lost some windows and a few pictures, but that's it," she said. "Why don't you come and stay with me until you find out whether you can move back in your rooming house?"

Gratefully, Kit accepted. It was at Nelly's kitchen table that the reporter wrote the earthquake story that would bring startling changes to her life.

EXCLUSIVE to the *Meadowridge Monitor*
FROM: Kathleen Ternan
DATE LINE: San Francisco, California, April 18, 1906

At 5:13 A.M. in the gray, foggy dawn of this April morning, disaster struck the beautiful city by the Bay. Citizens were awakened, roused out of sound sleep by a terrible rumbling noise followed by a series of strong, jolting shocks. Buildings toppled and walls crumbled. Falling bricks and beams smashed into the sidewalks. Huge craters opened in the streets. Telephone and telegraph poles crashed down, splintering onto tangles of wires and cutting off the city from the outside world for hours. Unless you saw it for yourself, you cannot imagine the extent of nature's destruction on this city.

Many reporters were covering the fires and the destruction of well-known mansions, restaurants, and commercial buildings. But it was the stories of the people that interested Kit the most. Every day, she ventured out to gather more material for her reports. There were many stories of missing family members and happier ones of reunions. Even with all the confusion, Kit learned of great acts of courage and kindness done for strangers. Bankers stood in food lines with carpenters, housemaids with their mistresses. And over and over, the reporter heard people say, "This changes your priorities. You learn what's really important."

On Friday Kit set out with her press card, hoping she could get past the downtown barriers to see for herself what remained of the business section and the mansions on Nob Hill.

Her blue straw hat with the cluster of violet flowers had almost become her signature. She wore it everywhere.

Today, a slight breeze was blowing in from the Bay. Thankfully, only a few smoldering pockets of fire remained here and there.

"Please, sir," she addressed the tired-looking policeman leaning against the wooden barricade. "I'm a reporter. I'd like to get in to cover the damage."

Before the policeman could answer, Kit heard her name.

"Kit! Kit Ternan!"

She whirled around to see a man in a stained white jacket running toward her. He had rumpled dark hair, brown stubble on his chin, and looked as though he hadn't slept in days. Within seconds, Kit realized it was Dan!

"Oh, Dan!" Kit wiped her eyes with one hand after their hug. "I'm so glad to see you!"

"Kit. Kit. I was so worried about you."

He placed both of his hands on either side of her face and kissed her on the mouth. When it ended, he chuckled. "This hat gave you away! I see you're still attached to it."

Kit's hand automatically went up to it. "It's a little worse for the wear, I think." She smiled.

"I had to find you," Dan said. "I was on my way toward Market Street when I spotted the hat."

The two friends quickly caught up on what had been happening to them.

"I've been ordered to get some sleep," Dan said at last. "We're quartered in the barracks at the fort. I have to go back on duty soon."

A month later, Dan was sitting in Nelly Armstrong's kitchen, reading one of Kit's articles. He had been so busy, he had not had time to read them earlier. Now on his day off, he had the chance.

"They're good, Kit. Really good. You're quite a writer."

Kit lifted the coffeepot from the stove and refilled his mug. "Wait until I tell you some exciting news," she said. "Some newspapers back East picked up a number of my stories. You know the woman's magazine *Woman's Hearth and Home*? Well, the editor wrote me and asked if I'd be interested in doing a series of articles for them. She said, and I quote, 'We'd like to see the same kind of heart-tugging interest stories you did in your series on the San Francisco earthquake.'"

Kit paused then said, "I think my career is taking off, Dan!"

"Congratulations! This *is* good news. You'll have no trouble getting your job back at the *Monitor* now." He grinned. "You're a celebrity in Meadowridge, you know."

Kit looked at him in surprise. "But I have no plans to get my old job back, Dan."

Dan reached across the plaid tablecloth and clasped her hand in his. "Let's go home, Kit."

She stared at him.

"Dr. Woodward's contacted me again," Dan went on. "He wants me to join his practice. He's made me a generous offer, Kit. You know I always wanted to be a country doctor. This would mean stepping into an established practice. It's a great opportunity."

Kit didn't know what to say. She could feel her emotions churn. "I'm happy for you, Dan."

"Didn't you hear what I said, Kit?" He leaned forward. "I want *us* to go home. You and me. Together!"

"I don't under—"

"Don't you realize I've fallen in love with you? I think I've actually loved you for a long time, Kit, only I didn't know it. I want us to get married and go back to Meadowridge together."

Kit's pulse began to pound.

"I always thought we were just good friends."

"That's the best kind of love, Kit, to begin as good friends." Dan smiled, but his eyes were serious. "So, what do you say?"

Longing for him swept through her like a strong Bay wind. She had given up any hope of his ever loving her years ago.

"Kit, you're everything I want in a woman," Dan pleaded. "You're brave and kind and smart and beautiful. I want you to share my life."

Kit had never allowed her true feelings for Dan to surface, and she wasn't sure she could release them now. She had kept them tucked away in her heart, convinced he loved Laurel.

Dan persisted, "What is it, Kit? Something's troubling you. Is it the thought of being a country doctor's wife?"

Kit shook her head. "No, it isn't that." She took a deep breath. "What about Laurel, Dan? I know you've always loved her."

Dan hesitated. "I *did* love Laurel, Kit. But loving her was part of growing up. She was a part of my life during school and so were you. Besides," he paused, "Laurel never did love me. I know that now.

"Over these past months, Kit, my feelings for you have been growing. They just needed time and tending. What I feel for you is the kind of love that lasts a lifetime. How can I convince you that I love you?"

"I do believe you, Dan, but I don't know. I don't know if I'm ready." Her eyes lowered, unable to meet his. "I don't know if I want to go back to Meadowridge. It took so long, and I worked so hard to get away." Her eyes met his. "I want to write, Dan. And I don't know if I can marry you and write too."

"A writer can write anywhere."

"It's not just the place. It's the time and energy. My heart would be divided—"

"You don't have to give me an answer right away, Kit." Dan got up. "I don't finish at the hospital until August, and Doc Woodward isn't expecting me until September. Take all the time you need. Just please don't say no."

19

Throughout the next busy months, San Franciscans set about to rebuild their city. The signs of construction were everywhere. Hammers banged nails into lumber, men in denims climbed up towering beams, the clinking of iron against iron at the blacksmith filled the air. Businesses reopened from the Bay to the country. Banks, restaurants, shops, and flower vendors each pulled up their shutters and unfurled their canvas awnings for customers. The city was coming back to life.

Night after night, Kit Ternan tossed and turned. Her thoughts kept her awake. What should she do? She longed to be cherished and cared for by someone like Dan. It was what she wanted. But she also wanted to write, to describe and share her thoughts, to report on events. How could she reach her goals as Dan's wife?

During these late-night sessions, an idea for a story kept haunting her like a recurring dream.

Dan encouraged her to write it. "It will touch a lot of people, Kit. It's your story. No one else can tell it the way you can. You'll be writing it for Toddy and Laurel and all the children who were on the Orphan Train."

Night after night, with the oil lamp burning low, Kit emptied her heart through her pen. Writing of her experiences as an abandoned child was difficult, but Kit trudged on. As she did, she came to understand the heartbreak of a young widowed father who had no other choice but to give up his three children. When she finished, she titled her story "Little Lost Family" and mailed it to *Woman's Hearth and Home*.

During the days, Kit continued working as a reporter for the *Times*. Every afternoon, she hurried back to her apartment on Market Street to check her mailbox for a response. Weeks went by with no word.

In September, Dan had returned to Meadowridge to take up practice with Dr. Woodward, and she missed him terribly. "I'm willing to wait," he told her as he kissed her good-bye.

Late one night, Kit wrote in her journal, "How can a city filled with people and noise and endless activity be such a lonely place because one person is missing?"

Finally, one day when she unlocked her box, a long white envelope with *WH&H* in the upper left-hand corner caught her eye. She ripped it open, and a check drifted to her feet. She opened the folded letter and read:

Dear Miss Ternan,

Your latest submission brought many a tear to our editorial staff. We would like to run it as the lead story in our December issue. I think it will bring a warm response from our readers. We are looking forward to having you as a regular contributor to our magazine and to receiving more of these heartwarming articles.

Kit's instant reaction was to tell Dan. But Dan wasn't here. Her excitement faded. That night, old memories haunted her: the day Da had left them at the orphanage; nights of lying in the narrow cot feeling abandoned; fears that no one would adopt her on the Orphan Train; long nights alone in the attic at the Hansen farm.

You could have gone back to Arkansas with Dan, she told herself. Right now you could be in his arms. What good is success if there is no one to share it?

Kit celebrated Christmas with Nelly and some of the folks from the *Times*. Dan sent her a leather writing portfolio, one that could be placed comfortably on her lap. In the card he had written: "Just to remind you that it's possible to write anywhere, even on a train to Meadowridge."

At the end of January, she received another letter from *Woman's Hearth and Home*. "The response to your story has been staggering," it read. "The magazine has been deluged with letters asking for reprints. These letters are being mailed under separate cover."

That very afternoon, a large manila envelope was dropped outside Kit's apartment door. It contained dozens of letters to Kit in care of the magazine. Kit poured the contents out on the table and pulled up a chair to read. The signature at the bottom of one note surprised and pleased her:

> I've just read a reprint of your beautiful story in our newspaper. You have succeeded, Kit, and I'm very proud of you.
>
> Your friend,
> Millicent Cady

There was more to come. Within a week Kit received another forwarded letter. As she opened the fine gray stationery, a small photograph fell out. It was a beautiful young woman in a wedding dress. Puzzled, Kit read:

My dear Miss Ternan,

You do not know me, but I have just finished reading your wonderful article. I knew I had to write you. After ten years with no children, my husband and I adopted a beautiful two-year-old baby girl from Greystone Orphanage in Boston. She was adorable with big blue eyes and masses of ringlets. We raised her in an atmosphere of love. Just after adopting Gwynny, my husband took over the management of another mill and we left Boston. In this new situation, everyone thought Gwynny was our own. We have never told her any different. She has done well. She sings and plays the harp. Last year she married a fine young man who practices law. I have not given you her married name or address because I'm sure it would be very disturbing for her to learn that she is adopted. I hope and pray that you will understand. God bless you, my dear. My heart was deeply touched by your suffering.

The letter was signed "A Christian Mother."

With tears in her eyes, Kit read the letter over and over. She examined each detail of the picture. Yes, in the eyes, the curls around the forehead, the dimples around her mouth, Kit could see the resemblance to her long-lost baby sister.

When all Kit's tears had been shed, she pulled her writing portfolio out of the closet. Dipping her pen in a bottle of ink, she began to write. It was time at last. The words flowed easily. When she finished, she signed the note, blotted it, addressed an envelope, and stamped it.

With a kiss, she folded the letter and placed it inside. So eager was she to post it that she threw on her brown wool coat and tam and ran down to the mailbox on the corner. The letter was addressed to Dr. Daniel Brooks of Meadowridge.

20

Kit was eagerly packing her trunk when Mrs. Bredesen knocked at the door.

"The mailboxes are jammed, Kit, so I thought I'd bring this up. You sure get a lot of mail!" The earthquake had improved the landlady's disposition considerably. She was almost pleasant.

"Thank you, Mrs. Bredesen," Kit replied.

Inside the envelope was a letter from Ava Woodward. The Woodwards were overjoyed about the news of her engagement to Dan and wanted Kit to stay with them until the wedding. Doctor Woodward offered to give her away.

"You know you are very special to us, like one of our own," Ava wrote in beautiful script. "You, Laurel, and Toddy are like sisters. We have some special surprises in store. Please allow us to do this for you."

Dr. Woodward had added a P.S. in his own hand: "Dan's condition is quite alarming. He wanders around Meadowridge forgetting things and staring into space. If I didn't know better, I'd examine him for an illness. But having suffered the same ailment myself thirty-some years ago, I easily recognize it. There is only one cure, and her name is Kathleen Ternan."

The train chugged up the last incline before dipping down into the valley. For the first time in three years, Kit caught sight of Meadowridge. The town lay nestled in the rolling hills, brilliant with fall colors. Its rooftops gleamed in the fall sunshine, and the church's steeple spiked up into the blue autumn sky.

At last, the train pulled to a stop at the yellow frame depot. As the whistle pierced the air, Kit sat on the edge of her seat and saw Dan waiting on the platform.

"Meadowridge! Meadowridge!" the conductor announced, swinging his gold watch fob in one hand.

"Kit, you're here! You're finally here!" Dressed in a blue suit and matching gloves, Kit held on to her hat as she flew into Dan's waiting arms.

Fresh coffee and piping hot cinnamon rolls awaited them at the Woodwards. After greeting each other, they gathered around the dining room table to discuss the wedding plans.

Dan couldn't keep his eyes off Kit. It had been so long, and he had missed her terribly. Although he had given her time to make her decision, he hadn't realized how lonely Meadowridge would be without her.

"Well, Dan." Dr. Woodward got to his feet at last. "I think we should leave the ladies to settle the details. We have patients to see."

After the two men left, Ava squeezed Kit's hand. "I can't tell you what it means to have you here. And I have wonderful news. Laurel is coming from Boston for the wedding. We hope she'll sing. Mrs. Hale wants to hold the reception at her home, and she's written Toddy."

Ava left Kit in the guest bedroom down the hall from Laurel's room. As Kit walked by her friend's empty room, she could almost hear the chatter and laughter from the years gone by. The flowered carpet and rose wallpaper reminded her of molasses cookies and lemonade and the time Laurel had confided in her about going to Boston. As Kit glanced into the half-open door, she remembered Laurel's remark: Nothing makes up for being an orphan.

Of course nothing feels like being abandoned as a child, but God can heal the pain and restore life and love if given the chance.

That evening after dinner with the Woodwards, Dan and Kit took a long walk. In the lingering light of the early autumn evening, they ended up at the Meadowridge Grammar School playground.

"It seems like a dream to be back here," Kit said as she swung idly in an old leather swing. "This brings back memories, doesn't it?"

"Yes, but I'd rather look forward to our future. I didn't think it was possible to be this happy." Dan twisted his swing around so he faced her. "I love you so much, Kit." He drew a small box from his coat pocket and placed it in Kit's hand. "Open it," he directed.

Inside the round velvet box, a single pearl shimmered against a dark blue lining. Kit drew in her breath.

"I wasn't sure what kind of engagement ring to get, but when I saw the pearl, I knew." He slipped it on her finger. "It's like you, Kit, pure and beautiful."

That night in the Woodwards' guest room, Kit slipped onto her knees. "Dear Lord," she prayed. "You *are* redeeming the heartache of my youth. In a lot of ways, I think Dan's love for me is making up for my having been an orphan. I know you've brought him into my life. Help me to be a good wife. And Lord, thank you."

Not long after her arrival, Kit and Dan rode out to the Hansen farm to see Cora and to pick up Ginger. Kit was grieved by what she saw. While the yard and the farmhouse looked much the same, Cora had declined greatly. Her skin was white, and her thin wispy hair barely covered her head. The elderly woman sat slumped in a chair but did not speak.

"She's not in any pain, Kit," Dan told her as they rode back into town. "Her daughter-in-law is taking good care of her. Whether or not she showed it, I'm sure it pleased her to see you."

With Ginger in her arms, Kit watched the hills and meadows flow by. How often she had ridden this road. How many times she had traipsed through these meadows and woods. How far she had come since that first trip with Jess to the farm. How much things in her life had changed.

"I wish I could have done more. I wish I could have done more to make her happy," Kit murmured as she stroked her cat's golden fur.

"You can't be responsible for another person's happiness, Kit. You did more than you know to make Cora Hansen's life brighter." He reached for her hand and drew it through one arm. "You do that for everyone whose life you touch."

Two days before the wedding, Laurel arrived. The friends hugged, laughing and crying and exclaiming all at once. They dashed up the polished staircase to talk.

"You look wonderful! Prettier than ever!" declared Kit.

"And you, Kit. You were always beautiful! But now—Love! If they could only bottle it and sell it, it would make someone a fortune!"

Later, while getting ready for bed, Kit sat at the dressing table in Laurel's room in front of the oval mirror. Putting down the hairbrush, she turned and looked her friend squarely in the eye.

"The truth, Laurel."

"The truth? Of course," Laurel replied. "What's the question?"

"I know you loved Dan once—"

"Yes, I did care for him. And I still do! But not like you think." She smiled. "I love him like a sister loves a brother."

"No regrets?"

"Oh, no, Kit," Laurel exclaimed. "If only you knew Gene. He's so wonderful. If it hadn't been for him, I wouldn't have found my father's paintings. He's helped me piece my life together in so many ways.

"God had it all planned, Kit," she said quietly. "You know, I remember that night at our graduation dance. I saw the way you looked at Dan. And now I see how Dan looks at you! You two love one another."

Kit wiped a tear from her cheek. "You knew?"

"Yes." Laurel leaned over and gave her friend a big hug. "And it was all right."

Suddenly Kit remembered. "Oh, Laurel, I haven't told you what happened after my article was published in *Woman's Hearth and Home!*"

As Kit was telling her about the letter from the woman who had adopted Gwynny, the bedroom door burst open.

"Surprise!"

Startled, Kit whirled around from the dressing table, and Laurel jumped.

"Toddy!" they both screamed.

The following afternoon while Laurel practiced her wedding solo at home in the parlor, Toddy and Kit walked over to decorate the church. Both the Woodwards' garden and Olivia Hale's gardener had supplied an abundance of brilliant fall flowers for the ceremony.

"I know you must still miss Helene," Kit said as she tied a satin white and gold ribbon in a bow on the end of a pew.

"I do," Toddy replied. It was still hard for her to think about her adopted sister's death. "We always knew. Her health was so delicate. I guess I just never wanted to believe it would actually happen."

"In the end, life forces us to face some unpleasant things, doesn't it?"

"Yes." Toddy arranged a bow on the next pew. "Her death made me face what I wanted to do with my life. It prompted my decision to go into nursing."

"So, how's Arizona?" Kit snipped her shears in the air.

"I love Chris and I love nursing, Kit. I wouldn't want to be anywhere else." With that, Toddy picked up a box of ribbons and moved to the front of the church.

That evening, the three friends gathered in Laurel's room. They were all quiet, knowing this would be the last time they would be together for quite a while. Laurel's train would be leaving for Boston the day after the ceremony.

Toddy broke the silence, "Do you remember what we promised each other on the Orphan Train?"

"Of course!" Laurel hunched one shoulder up in the air, and Kit started dragging one foot and limping. A cross-eyed Toddy collapsed on the bed clutching her stomach from laughing.

"We promised we'd be friends forever," Kit finally managed to say.

"No matter what," Toddy added.

"And we will," Laurel said firmly. "We may be going our separate ways, but we'll always stay in touch. Always."

Morning sunlight streamed into the front bedroom. With her hands behind her head, Kit lay in bed thinking and dreaming. All of a sudden, tiny gray pebbles pelted the windowpane. She threw back her covers,

119

leaped up, and ran over to the half-open window. Below the window stood Dan.

"Daniel Brooks! What are you doing here?"

"I couldn't sleep!" He grinned.

Kit tried to scowl. "But we're not supposed to see each other before the wedding. It's tradition."

"I had to come." He made a helpless gesture. "I had to see if you were really here. Do you love me? Are you going to marry me today?"

"Yes, I love you. And yes, I'm going to marry you today! Just be there!"

Her groom blew her a kiss, and the young bride listened to him whistle as he went through the front gate. Kit loved his boyish charm and suddenly realized that her nervousness had vanished. Later, even Ava commented on how composed she looked.

At noon, Meadowridge Community Church overflowed with good friends. Laurel sang "The Lord's Prayer," and Toddy walked down the aisle as the matron of honor. At the first chords of the wedding march, smiling faces turned to watch the beautiful bride on the doctor's arm. Even Jess Hansen, dressed in a real tie, was there! His five boys and their families filled up the pew.

She, Kathleen Ternan, was wanted, accepted, loved. She had a family. She belonged.

The wind blowing through the open window was fragrant with the smell of new spring blossoms. Kit looked up from her desk at the *Meadowridge Monitor*. The town square was swarming with people today. Leaning her chin on her hand, she tapped her teeth with the tip of her short but sharp pencil and stole a short break.

When Dan's grandmother died, she had left him her house in Meadowridge not far from the Woodwards. The frame building, now painted white with light blue shutters was slowly but surely becoming their home as Kit decorated it room by room.

Kit was very happy being married to the man she loved. Since Dan was now taking over more of Dr. Woodward's patients, his hours were long. Thus, Kit had time to write without neglecting her new husband. She spent three afternoons a week at the *Monitor*.

"Mornin', Mizz Brooks." The postman's voice interrupted her thoughts. "I think you git more mail than anybody in these here parts!" He chuckled as he unraveled a stack of letters tied together with a string. "Here's more!"

Kit shuffled through the envelopes. She was still receiving forwarded letters from the magazine. Her article had truly touched the hearts of many people. But there was one place it hadn't reached. The thought of Kit's father and brother still tapped into a well of sadness deep within her own soul. She still held on to the hope of finding them. Perhaps one day . . .

A short while later, Kit was working on an article for the next issue. She did not glance up when she heard the front door open. It was probably only Mr. Clooney, who often came in and out. Bent over her desk, Kit did not look up until a shadow crossed her desk. She lifted her head.

The man whipped off a battered tweed cap.

With her reporter's eye, Kit scanned the stranger quickly. Sandy-colored hair framed the man's weather-beaten face. Of medium height, he wore a rough blue cotton shirt open at the neck, a sleeveless plaid vest, and faded pants. His unpolished boots were scratched and the toes scraped.

"'Scuse me, miss, but are you Miss Ternan?"

"Yes," Kit replied.

With the cap tucked under one arm, the stranger reached into a pocket on his vest. The knuckles on his calloused hands were swollen and scarred. He pulled out a piece of paper, carefully folded. Slowly, his big fingers unfolded it and held it up, his broken nails clearly visible. "You wrote this?"

Kit recognized a worn copy of her article "Little Lost Family." She nodded her head.

"Well, Kit, it's me—Jamie."

Stunned, Kit stared at him. "Jamie?" she repeated.

"The same." He grinned.

A torrent of feelings rushed over her. *Jamie!* Her little lost brother. Here in the flesh! After all these years and all the hope and all the prayers.

The pencil in Kit's fingers snapped. Her chair crashed to the floor as she jumped up. "Jamie! Oh, Jamie!" she cried. "How did you find me?"

"I was in St. Louis, and I seen this in the newspaper. Couldn't hardly believe the story was 'bout us, Kit."

"Oh, Jamie, this is so wonderful! To think you found me when I've been praying for so long to find you!" Tears streamed down her face.

Kit held out both hands to him. "We have so much to talk about, Jamie, to catch up on. You must come home with me. I want you to meet my husband."

"You're married? But the byline says Ternan."

"That's my professional name, the name I write under. My husband's a doctor, and we live just a few blocks over."

She bent over to pick up the chair and retrieve her light sweater draped over the back. She tucked her arm through her newfound brother's. "I have so much to ask you," she began as she pushed the front door open. "So many questions."

"I was adopted by a nice old couple who didn't have any kids," Jamie told her as he cut into the large piece of apple pie on his plate. "They had a little farm upstate. I stayed with 'em three years." He swallowed a bite. "Went to a little country school and even had a pony to ride. He was black and white too. Had chores to do every day. I liked it jest fine." He paused and leaned his elbows on the table while he ate. "I guess you could say that was the end of the good times."

"What do you mean?"

"Well, the old man died and a neighbor, name of Gordon, bought out the old lady. He got me in the bargain. He didn't care nothin' 'bout kids though. Jest wanted extra hands," he added glumly. "I should'a run away right then."

"Why did the lady let you go?"

"Said she was goin' to live with her sister, who had four kids. She cried somethin' awful though. I don't think she wanted to leave me." The coffee cup clinked the saucer as he put it down.

"Talk 'bout mean, Kit." Jamie shook his head. "If I was to take off my shirt, you'd see the scars 'cross my back where he used a buggy whip." He shrugged. "I was just a scrawny kid. What could I do 'gainst a growed man?"

Kit let her coffee get cold. "What *did* you do?"

"Run away. Me and another kid workin' for 'im. Caught the freight train when it slowed for the crossin'."

"You rode the freight cars?"

"Plenty of times." He curled his thick fingers around the handle of the cup and picked it up. "It weren't that bad." He took a sip. "T'were other guys there too. But me and Tom, we stuck together."

"No school?"

"Nope. But I got along. One summer Tom and me got a job with a carney. You know, a travelin' carnival. Liked it so much I stayed with it. I git to see a lot of the country. It ain't such a bad life."

Kit's heart ached. Her little brother had been so bright, so quick. If only he could have gotten an education as she had. If only he could have known love as she had. If only . . .

Just then, the back door flung open. It was Dan, who warmly welcomed their surprise visitor. The rest of the evening, Jamie shared about his life as a carney roustabout. Since Dan had surgery scheduled for the next morning, he turned in early. Kit tossed some large pillows on the floor, and she and her brother settled down in front of the fireplace, where a small fire now glowed.

"This is Gwynny's picture," she told him, showing him the letter from Gwynny's adoptive mother too.

"I'm glad things turned out good for her." He handed the picture back to her.

Then, a strange long silence fell between them. At last, Jamie said, "I found Da, Kit."

Kit shook her head in disbelief.

"Did you say you found Da?"

"Yeh. I found our 'doption papers in my stuff when I went to Gordon's. Da's name and address was on 'em. I took a chance he was still in Brockton."

"Did you see him?"

For a moment, she could almost see her father's sad face the night he had talked to her at the kitchen table. The memory of that day he had taken them to Greystone came back in all its pain.

"Yeah." Jamie's voice was gruff. "I went by his house and seed some kids outside. I figured he wouldn't be too happy 'bout another kid showin' up on his doorstep, so I waited outside the shoe factory."

"Did you speak to him?"

"He didn't know me. I was pretty big, even at fourteen. He got kinda pale. Stumbled around that he was married now with some kids—"

"Did he ask about Gwynny and me?" was Kit's next question.

Jamie looked embarrassed and shook his head. "I think he felt bad about deserting all of us, but—" her brother shrugged. "Poor guy. I guess he was up against a wall— out of work, four mouths to feed. Who's to say what he should have done."

Kit reached over and squeezed Jamie's big rough hand. "I guess there's nothing to do but forgive him, Jamie."

The clock on the mantel struck two before they finally said good night. Kit hugged him. "I hope you'll stay for a while, Jamie."

"Thanks, Kit," he replied.

The next morning, the room was full of sunshine when Kit woke up. She had overslept! Tying the sash of her robe, she rushed downstairs. "Jamie!" she called. No one answered. The downstairs bedroom door was open, the sheets and blankets neatly folded at the foot of the bed.

"Jamie!" she called. There was no answer.

As she entered the parlor, she saw a folded paper on the mantel, propped against the clock.

Dear Kit,

It was sure grate to see ya. I had to ketch a trane to were the carney is playin nex weke. Don't be sad. Now I know were you are. I'll cum back.

Your bruther,
Jamie
P.S. You got a fine husband. Tell him so long for me.

Kit slipped the note into her bathrobe pocket, went into the kitchen, and filled the kettle with water. Before she knew what was happening, great racking sobs erupted from deep within her.

With her face in her hands, she cried. She wept for Jamie, for herself, for Gwynny, and for Da. She grieved for all the years they might have had together as a family and for what they had lost. She mourned for all the letters she had written and for all of her dashed hopes. She sobbed because she had finally found her little lost brother. God had answered her prayer.

Slowly, the storm of her emotions passed, and a kind of calm settled over her.

As Kit sat at her new kitchen table in her new home, she realized she had needed to cry those tears for a very long time. It was natural to grieve for what had been lost. She had discovered that her younger brother had found peace in his life, that her baby sister was happy. This was what counted.

And Kit was happy too. She now understood that everything for her own joy was right in front of her. God had turned everything that had been bad in her life around to good.

Kit spent the morning planting tomatoes and squash and cucumbers for a summer vegetable garden. That afternoon she read a favorite book of poetry, something she hadn't done for a long time. For dinner, she fixed a chicken casserole and mixed salad and placed yellow jonquils in a blue willow pitcher that had belonged to Dan's grandmother.

She had just done her hair and put on a fresh blouse when she heard footsteps on the porch.

"Kit, Kit! I'm home!" Dan called as he stepped inside.

Kit ran down the stairs to greet him. "So am I, Dan. So am I."

About the Author

I grew up in a small Southern town, in a home of story-tellers and readers, where authors were admired and books were treasured and discussed. When I was nine years old, an accident confined me to bed. As my body healed, I spent hours at a time making up stories for my paper dolls to act out. That is when I began to write stories.

As a young woman, three books had an enormous impact on me: *Magnificent Obsession, The Robe,* and *Christy.* From these novels I learned that stories held the possibility of changing lives. I wanted to learn to write books with unforgettable characters who faced choices and challenges and were so real that they lingered in readers' minds long after they finished the book.

The Orphan Train West for Young Adults series is especially dear to my heart. I first heard about these orphans when I read an *American Heritage* magazine story titled "The Children's Migration." The article told of the orphan trains taking more than 250,000 abandoned children cross country to be placed in rural homes. I knew I had to write some of their stories. Toddy, Laurel, Kit, Ivy and Allison, and April and May are all special to me. I hope you will grow to love them as much as I do.

Jane Peart lives in Fortuna, California, with her husband, Ray.

The Orphan Train West for Young Adults Series

They seek love with new families . . . and turn to God to find ultimate happiness.

The Orphan Train West for Young Adults series provides a glimpse into a fascinating and little-known chapter of American history. Based on the actual history of hundreds of orphans brought by train to be adopted by families in America's heartland, this delightful series will capture your heart and imagination.

Popular author Jane Peart brings the past to life with these heartwarming novels set in the 1800s, which trace the lives of courageous young girls who are searching for fresh beginnings and loving families. As the girls search for their purpose in life, they find strength in God's unconditional love.

Follow the girls' stories as they pursue their dreams, find love, grow in their faith, and move beyond the sorrows of the past.

Look for the other books in the Orphan Train West for Young Adults series!

Left at Boston's Greystone Orphanage by her actress mother, exuberant Toddy sets out on the Orphan Train along with her two friends, Kit and Laurel. On the way, the three make a pact to stay "forever friends." When they reach the town of Meadowridge, Toddy joins the household of Olivia Hale, a wealthy widow who wants a companion for her delicate granddaughter, Helene. Before long, Toddy wins their hearts and brightens their home with her optimism and zest for life.

As the years pass, Toddy brings much joy to Helene and Mrs. Hale. Yet happiness eludes her. Is Toddy's yearning for a home only a dream?

LAUREL

Shy, sensitive Laurel is placed at Boston's Greystone Orphanage when her mother enters a sanitarium. After her mother's death, Laurel is placed on the Orphan Train with Kit and Toddy, destined for the town of Meadowridge. There she is adopted by Dr. and Mrs. Woodward, who still grieve for the daughter they lost two years earlier.

Laurel brings a breath of fresh air— and much love—into the Woodwards' home. As she grows up, though, Laurel longs to discover her true identity. Her search leads her to Boston, where she uncovers secrets from her past. But will Laurel's new life come between her and the love she desires?

IVY & ALLISON

Ivy Austin dreams about being adopted and leaving the orphanage, but when her life takes a strange turn, she ends up on the Orphan Train. There she meets Allison, whose pretty features and charm are sure to win her a new home. Worried that she will be overlooked by potential parents and not wanting to be left behind, Ivy acts impulsively.

As Ivy and Allison grow up together in the town of Brookdale, their past as insecure orphans still hurts, even though they have loving adoptive families. Their special friendship is a comfort, but is it strong enough to withstand the truth of Ivy's secret?